NOT
MY
LIFE

A Zachary Marchand Mystery
series book two

by Paulette D. Morrissey

Not My Life - A Zachary Marchand Mystery
Copyright 2015 by Paulette D. Morrissey
Tulip Square Books
Brookfield WI

Published by Tulip Square Books
First Edition
July 2015
ISBN: 978-942975-05-2
Also available as an ePub Book

Cover design by Paulette D. Morrissey

DEDICATION

This book is dedicated to my brother-in-law
David Guss. Without his helpful input and knowledge,
this book could not have been completed.

Other books written by the Author:

Dead Serious Day - A Zachary Marchand Mystery
Nyntahls - They're in Your House

Chapter 1

"Melody, please listen to reason. There's no need for you to do anything rash that we may both regret," Harold pleaded his case as he paced back and forth in their expansive living room.

Melody stood silently on the far side of the room, looking out the window across their beautifully manicured front lawn. The cobblestone pavers wove across the yard, framed by endless beds of flowers in all colors and sizes. It was a beautiful sight, and normally Melody loved looking at her gardens, but not today. She stared blankly out the window, trying to figure out what she should do. She was a very attractive woman, thirty-seven years old, and in good shape, partly due to the fact that she'd never bore any children, and never wanted to. She shook her head slightly, her shoulder length auburn hair waving slightly as she did. "I don't know what I want to do with my life Harold, but I'm pretty sure it doesn't include you, or any of this," she said flatly, motioning to the extravagant room and all its costly furnishings.

"All right, all right, I understand, we may have drifted apart. Can you give me a chance to make it up to you?" Harold pleaded as he moved closer. "Maybe we should have a baby. That could bring us closer."

"Please Harold, I need to think. I need to get away from here and think," Melody said, keeping her distance from him. "I think I want a divorce, you realize that, don't you? Having a baby is the last thing I'm thinking about."

"All right, but I'd like a chance to try and convince you not to go that route. Why don't you go up to the cabin this weekend. Clear your head a little, and when you come back, give me a week, one week, to change your mind," Harold said. "That's not too much to ask after eight years of marriage, is it? One more week? Then if I don't convince you we can make this work, I won't fight the divorce."

"All right, fine, I can do that," she said wearily, "I'm tired of fighting with you about this. I wouldn't mind a quiet few days up in the cabin alone. But one week Harold, that's all I'm waiting once I get back. One week. Seven days. After that, you tell all your lawyer friends that one of them is going to have to represent me in a divorce case," she said as she brushed past him and strode out of the room.

Harold stood there silently, clenching and unclenching his fists. He could feel the veins in his temples bulging. You bitch, he thought to himself, we'll see who wins this battle.

The couple didn't talk much to each other for the next few days. Harold stayed late at work most nights, snuck away to see his lady friend for a few hours, and pretty much avoided any more confrontations with Melody. He needed to stay married to her, at all costs. He'd do whatever he had to, to keep this marriage together.

For her part, Melody made plans to spend a quiet weekend at their rustic cabin on Green Lake, only a couple hours away. After that, she'd give Harold his week to make some pathetic attempt to mend their marriage, then she was ready to get a divorce and move on with her life. She was done with his cheating, his obsession with everything materialistic, wanting more of everything all the time. He was constantly trying to appease or please his iron-handed father who owned the law firm where Harold worked. She was tired of everyone else trying to run her life, telling her what she should do, what to wear, where to shop, who she should associate with. She wanted her simple life back. Her old friends, even her old job as office manager at a furniture company. How had she been so blind to marry Harold in the first place? Was he this bad when she met him? She didn't think so, but didn't remember anymore. All she knew was he was trying to make her into someone she wasn't. And she was done letting that happen. She breathed a sigh of relief as she packed a small overnight bag on Friday afternoon. She was looking forward to a quiet weekend alone, where she could start planning her new life. But she never made it to Green Lake.

Chapter 2

The morning sun was bright as it filtered through the thin lace hanging at the windows. The two long French windows were open, allowing a delicious breeze to rustle the lacy curtains ever so slightly as it crossed the room. With a sleepy yawn, she stretched and forced herself out of her slumber. Half asleep, she slowly opened her eyes, while enjoying the cool breeze across her face. The silky sheets that surrounded her made it difficult to want to leave the bed.

And then she bolted upright, instantly awake! She didn't have silk sheets, and she never left the window open at night! She looked anxiously around the room, a panicky feeling growing inside her. This wasn't her bed, or her bedroom! Where was she? She turned slightly and was shocked to see a man sleeping next to her in the bed. Who was he? She had no husband, boyfriend or significant other. She let out a gasp as she jumped from the bed and fell on the floor in a tangle of silk sheets and bedding.

"Well, good morning, Melody, did you sleep well?" A quiet voice spoke to her from the bed.

"Who are you? Where am I?" She was unable to keep the panic from her voice, as she wrapped herself in the jumbled bedding and scooted backward slightly, "and what did you just call me?"

"Melody, take it easy, it's me, Harold, your husband, remember?" He spoke softly and slowly in a very calm voice, "take your time, it will come back to you."

"You aren't my husband. I'm not married! My name's not Melody. What is going on here?" She looked at this stranger, her eyes wide open.

"You were in a car accident Melody, do you remember that? You were on your way to spend a few days at the cabin, and your car was hit by a pickup truck. You hit your head pretty hard and were banged up pretty good. Things are going to be jumbled up for you for awhile," Harold said as he sat up in bed.

"I think I remember something about an accident," she said, "but I'm still not Melody. I don't know any Melody. My name is… I can't think right now, but I don't know you, or this bedroom or any of this, and you are surely not my husband!"

Harold made a move to get out of the bed and come toward her, but she would have none of that. Quickly she got to her feet, and promptly almost passed out.

"Easy, you aren't supposed to be jumping around like that yet," Harold said as he gently helped her up and back onto the bed. "You were only released yesterday, let's take it a little slower."

She reluctantly sat on the edge of the bed and took a few deep breaths. What was happening? What did this Harold guy think he was doing? She tried to remember the accident and the hospital. She reached up to rub her hands across her head and was startled to feel bandages on her face.

"What's wrong with my face?" She screamed as her hands felt all over her face and head. "Where's a mirror? What happened to me?"

"Please, Melody. I wish you could calm down for just a minute," Harold coaxed her as he gave her a small hand mirror. "We go through all of this every day. You were in an accident a little over a week ago. You hit your head pretty bad, which is why your memory is a mess. You needed a little repair on your face. Your nose was broken, your cheek cut open and you had a pretty big gash across your forehead that required stitches. All the bandages come off soon and the stitches come out and you'll be good as new. You looked a lot worse a week ago, believe me. Two black eyes, busted lip, all bruised up."

"I don't think so," she said as she stared in the mirror. She knew she was looking at herself, but she didn't look quite right. Did she really bang her head that hard?

"You don't think so, what?" Harold was puzzled.

"I don't think I'll be good as new. Something is really wrong here." She turned away from the mirror and as she shifted in the bed a little she noticed the cast on her foot. No wonder she fell out of bed. "Did I break my foot in the accident too?"

"Yes, yes you did. I thought you were aware of that."

"Anything else? Internal bleeding, other broken bones? Ribs maybe? Ruptured spleen, what?" She angrily said as she felt around on her body.

"No, I don't think so. Like I said, you were bruised up, and you were in the hospital for a week, mostly due to your head injuries, but you were thoroughly checked over," Harold sounded almost amused by her confusion.

"Look, I think there's been a really big mistake. I'm not your wife. This is all a mistake. I vaguely recall being in an accident, and being put in an ambulance. But after that, you have this all wrong. Maybe I look like your wife, but you must know I'm not her," she calmed down a little and tried to make him understand.

"Mel, listen to me. We have had this conversation about a hundred times. Dr. Mathias has been caring for you. He'll be by to see you later. Little by little you'll start to remember your life, and remember who you are, who I am, and it will all come back to you. We live here, in Delafield, in Wisconsin. You are my wife, your name is Melody Richardson and we've been married close to eight years. Some of my family are coming over tonight to see how you're doing. They've all been worried sick about you. Maybe you'll remember one or two of them," Harold said as he tried to put an arm around her as he sat next to her on the bed.

As he spoke, she could vaguely remember him, and the smell of his cologne. Could he be right? She wondered as he patiently repeated his story to her. No, her name wasn't Melody. It was…
..damn, why couldn't she remember her own name? She shook her head violently, as if to clear away the cobwebs inside.

"Don't, don't. You have to take it easy yet," he gently pushed her back onto the pillows. "I'm going to give you a pill that Dr. Mathias prescribed, it will help you relax, alright? Will you take it? It won't make you sleep if you don't want to, just calm you a little. Then we can talk more." He handed her a small blue tablet that he shook from the bottle on the nightstand, and gave her a drink of water. Reluctantly, she took it, unsure if she should trust this man.

"I don't think I can stay here. I don't belong here, don't you understand what I'm saying?" She tried again to get through to him.

"Let's just give it some time, you'll start to remember things soon, I promise," he said as he patted her on the head like a child, then gently prodded, "try to remember, do you remember me? Look at me, surely you remember me, we've been together for eight years."

"I think I might vaguely remember you, a little maybe, but I don't know. I'm not married to you. I'm not Melody," she insisted as she allowed herself to be laid back onto the pillows. Before too long, she was sound asleep and Harold quietly left the room.

When she woke up later that afternoon, Harold was sitting on the side of the bed and there was another man in the room standing over her. She gave a startled gasp.

"It's ok, Mel, this is Dr. Mathias, do you remember him? He's been caring for you since the accident," Harold said softly.

"No, I don't think, but maybe. I'm all confused," she said, shaking her head ever so slightly. "And please stop calling me Melody, would you?"

"What would you like me to call you, my dear?" Harold asked, attempting to hold her hand.

"I don't know. Nothing," she said with a deep sigh. "Are you taking off all these bandages, doctor?"

"That I am, Mel…" Dr. Mathias said, unsure of what to call her. "I think it's time for some stitches to come out too."

He worked quickly and painlessly, removing all her bandages, and then snipping a number of stitches from various places on her face. "You have a bit of swelling and light bruising yet, but that will all go away soon enough. It all looks great, I don't think you'll have any visible scars. Want to have a look?"

"Yes, I think so," she said, taking the hand mirror he offered. Carefully she studied her face, turning her head slightly from side to side. Frowning a bit when she was finished with her scrutiny. "I look different. I mean it's me, but a little different."

"Well, like I said, the swelling isn't gone completely, and some extensive surgery was needed on your broken nose and your cheek bone. You took quite a hit. You might not look 100% the same as before, but I'd guess it's 95%. Another week or so and you won't even notice the slight changes," Dr. Mathias said in a soothing voice. "You have several stitches that will dissolve on their own, so if I leave the bandages off, you must not play with them, all right?" He spoke as if she were a scared child, said his goodbyes and left.

"Do you feel like getting up a bit, or would you prefer to rest some more?" Harold asked as he tried to pat her hand again.

She pulled her hand away, crossed her arms and tucked her hands into her armpits. "I guess I'd like to get up a while, I'm tired of lying here, but what am I supposed to do?"

"Let me get you a dressing gown to put on, and we can go downstairs and have Marjorie fix you a late lunch," Harold offered.

"Do I know who Marjorie is?" she asked as she watched him walk to the closet on the other side of the large room and return with a very silky luxurious robe. She let him help her into it, and eased herself out of bed. Reluctantly, she took his arm to steady herself.

"Marjorie is our cook, perhaps you'll remember her. I'm sure you'll remember her great cooking!" He chuckled as he helped her down the hall and carefully down the wide, grandiose staircase.

She said nothing, just allowed herself to be led through the house to the dining room. She was stunned by the size of each room, and all the exquisite furnishings. There were beautiful paintings on the walls, polished hardwood trim framing the rooms, stunning rugs on the polished marble floors and beautiful, antique furniture everywhere. She didn't know what to think. Was this really her home? Was she really Harold's wife? Harold, Harold, she was starting to remember him, she thought. Maybe he was her husband after all. Everything was so fuzzy and confusing, as if she could almost remember things, but not quite.

Harold pulled out a richly upholstered chair at the huge dining table and seated her, then went off to fetch Marjorie. He returned quickly with a heavyset Hispanic woman who came in wringing her hands and all anxious to get close to her.

"Ma'am, I am so happy to see you up and about! We have all been so worried about you! What a scare you gave us all!" she clucked away endlessly as she gave her a quick hug, then clasped her hands in front of her ample bosom. "You are looking very good after such a terrible thing! What can I get for you my dear? Your favorite sandwich and soup, or would you like something else?"

"Um, sure...what is my favorite sandwich and soup?" she asked shyly.

"Why it's an egg salad sandwich on marble rye, and chicken noodle soup! Have you forgotten?" Marjorie chuckled and gave another quick hug, "bless your heart, you did take quite a knock in the head." Marjorie chuckled again as she left the room.

"Do you remember Marjorie?" Harold asked, taking a seat next to her.

"No, but she sure seems to know me, doesn't she?" she asked, her mind still trying to make sense of all of this.

"That she does, as we all do, you'll see. You enjoy your lunch with Marjorie, I have a few things to attend to. I'll be back to check on you soon," Harold said as he rose, planted a quick kiss on her forehead and left.

For the next hour or more, she spent an enjoyable if confusing time with Marjorie, who talked nonstop about her, the house, her marriage to Harold, his relatives, and anything else she could think of. Any questions she had, Marjorie was happy to fill in as many answers as she could. Though instead of reassuring her, all this information only confused her further. None of it seemed even vaguely familiar, with the exception of Harold himself. She seemed to remember him, if only a little. Marjorie took her through the house to see if anything would jog her memory, but nothing did, not even her supposed prized rose garden. Frustrated, she went back to her bed, dutifully took her little blue pill and went back to sleep.

When she woke a few hours later, Harold was by her side once again, coaxing her awake. She had visitors who were anxious to see her. He helped her to her feet and once again walked her downstairs.

"Mel, this is my father Ernest, my brother Thomas and his wife Rita. This is my sister Virginia and her husband Steven, and their son Kyle," Harold said as he walked her slowly into the room to sit on the sofa. "Seems a little odd to be introducing you to people you've known for years, but we do what we must do."

She politely smiled at each of them. "It's nice to meet you," she said lamely, not knowing exactly what was expected of her now.

Virginia broke the awkward silence. "Mel, we are all so happy to see you up and around! You looked so horrible in the hospital pictures Harold emailed us, I wondered if you'd ever be the same again. But here you are, as beautiful as ever! Maybe even more so. And the memory stuff will all come back, it takes time. And we are all here to help you! Even Kyle here, who loves his Aunt Melody, don't you Kyle?" she said as she gave her six year old son a gentle nudge.

"Hi Aunt Melody. I'm glad you're getting better. I made you a picture," the little boy said as he gave her a quick hug and presented her with the drawing he made.

"That's so sweet of you, thank you Kyle," she said, giving him a big hug in return, as she took the childish drawing he made for her.

"We are all happy for you Mel, now that you are on the road

to recovery," Ernest said in a deep strong voice, "now how about we all go have some of that delicious food of Marjorie's that I can smell from here."

Dinner was surprisingly comfortable and enjoyable, though it seemed odd to her to be eating with all these strangers as if they were her family. How strange a brain injury can do this, she told herself. No one else seemed to think anything was wrong. The first few minutes they made comments directed to her, but after that, it was normal dinner conversation for everyone. She didn't have much to say, but enjoyed the banter. She was even starting to feel just a tiny bit better about the whole situation.

Chapter 3

She lay quietly in bed the following morning, enjoying the stillness. Harold had already left the room and she was alone. Her mind seemed a little clearer, and she pushed to remember anything. Looking around the room, at all the belongings that were supposedly hers, she felt nothing. Carefully she went into the huge walk-in closet, that was the size of a large room. She gasped when she saw the amount of clothes in there! It looked like a department store. She pulled a few items off their hangers. They were all her size, but not the sort of clothes she thought she would wear. All were expensive silks and rayons, tailored and perfect looking. She tried on a pair of black slacks and a soft mohair sweater. They fit well, and she loved the feel of them, but it didn't feel like anything she'd worn before. Then a thought came into her mind - jeans! Where were all of her blue jeans? She went through the whole closet, looking in every drawer and on every shelf, but didn't find a single pair. She was still rummaging through all the clothes when Harold walked in.

"You're up! That's good to see, and you even got dressed today, you're making nice progress," he said with a smile.

"Where are all my jeans?" she said, noticing his smile looked rather forced. "I can't find a single pair of my jeans."

"Blue jeans? Denim? I don't think you own a pair of them, Mel. I can't recall ever seeing you in a pair of jeans," he furrowed his brow.

"I love jeans. I think I'm starting to remember a little, and I remember jeans," she said firmly, still going through the endless drawers.

"What on earth do you think I did with your jeans?" He said with a sharp chuckle, "run home and toss them all out while you were in the hospital?"

She ignored him, finished going through the closet, and walked out. She stood looking out the bedroom windows, wondering what the hell was going on. Something was tickling the back of her mind, wanting to come forward. She could almost feel it trying to work it's way into her consciousness. The jeans were only the beginning, there was a lot more to come, she knew it in her bones.

Then just like that, it happened. Like a flickering old filmstrip, she could suddenly picture things. Things that were familiar to her. Her apartment! Her bedroom! Her name!! She wasn't Melody, she was Elise! Elise Taggert, and this wasn't her home. In an instant, Elise remembered the little shops she walked to from her apartment, the park she jogged through most mornings. A feeling of terror immediately accompanied all these memories. If they were true, what was she doing here? Who was Melody and where was she? She turned to look at Harold, who was leaning in the closet doorway, arms folded across his chest.

"It's all coming back to me," she said hesitantly, wanting to see his reaction.

"It is? That's great," he said as he came a step closer.

"No, it isn't. I'm not remembering any of this," she said with a wave of her hand, "I'm remembering my real life."

"This is your real life, after a brain injury," he said, trying to sound calm, with an edge of annoyance barely concealed. "If you're remembering anything else, it's all false memories, created by your injured brain."

"No, this is all wrong! I can picture my apartment, the park I run in, the stores I shop in, a lot of things. You're telling me I'm imagining all of it? None of it exists?" She shook her head softly, not wanting to make herself dizzy.

"I understand what you're saying, but it's wrong. All those things about your apartment, your neighborhood, your whole life. Those are little bits and pieces of things you've seen, or read about or visited, and your jumbled up brain is trying to make sense of all your memories and it got some of them wrong. Dr. Mathias explained it like you have a box with hundreds of photographs in it from your life and you dropped that box and all the contents got mixed up. Then you're blindfolded and told to pick out the pictures that are your life. Without being able to see the pictures, you'd pick a bunch of random things that have nothing to do with each other. That's what your brain is doing - pulling random memories from your mind and trying to make them into a complete life that makes sense. Once your blindfold is removed, you can see you got it all wrong, but until then, you can't. So right now, we're just waiting for that blindfold to come off, so to speak." He spoke slowly as if he were explaining it to a child.

"So I'm just supposed to take your word for all of this, pretend I'm your wife, and then what?" She said, panic evident in her voice, "how can I do that when I know I'm not?"

"You met my family, you've talked to Marjorie, are they all pretending they know you? Is this all a giant conspiracy? And if you're not my wife, why would I be doing this?" He asked as he shook his head and left the room.

She stood in the middle of the room, unsure of what to do next. Finally she went downstairs to talk to Marjorie, who was working in the kitchen.

"Marjorie, do I seem the same to you? Is anything different?" she asked, not sure how to approach her.

"Ma'am, you seem fine to me! Better than ever even. I'm so happy to see you up and about again!" Marjorie clucked happily away.

"But am I different? I think something's wrong," she said, unsure of how much she should say to anyone connected to Harold.

"No, not really. You look like you lost a few pounds, but that's normal, lying in a hospital bed for more than a week, " Marjorie said, as she looked closer at Elise, "You look a little different, but you had some surgery done, so that's normal. Mostly, you look more refreshed, relaxed, that's all."

"All right, thanks Marjorie," She said, as she wandered out of the kitchen. She didn't know what to do next. She couldn't drive, with her right foot in a cumbersome cast, and didn't know where any car keys were if she could. She couldn't think of anyone to call. She had no family to speak of, at least none that she could remember. Who could she ask about Elise?

"Marjorie, do I have a laptop? Where would I keep it?" She asked.

"Yes ma'am you do, it's in your study, down the hall, just past the garden doors," Marjorie motioned with a smile.

She went quickly to the study, as expensively furnished as the rest of the house. Tall bookcases filled one wall, with mostly garden and flower books on all the shelves. Tastefully framed botanical prints hung on the walls. Two big comfy overstuffed floral chairs and an ottoman were tucked off to one side of the room, overlooking the garden, and on the other side stood a beautiful antique desk. The top of the desk was a rich burnished wood, worn to a soft, smooth patina over many years of use. The only things on the desk were a lamp, a framed photo of Harold and Melody, and the laptop. She quickly opened it and was dismayed to see it needed a password. She had no clue what the password might be, but was able to log in as a guest.

"Ok, where to start?" she said quietly, as she opened the browser. "What do I look up? The accident, my name, what?" She started by looking up Melody Richardson. There were numerous mentions of Melody on the society pages, some flower club page, and pictures of her and Harold at various functions. She gasped, as the pictures looked like they were of herself and Harold. The newest item she found was mention of the accident. It sounded like the same accident she vaguely remembered. A blue pickup truck ran a stop sign and slammed into her car. She suffered numerous facial injuries, a broken foot and a severe concussion. Next she looked up her own name, Elise Taggert. No mention of her on any society pages, nothing. She kept looking, then finally found it - there had been a fire in an apartment building in Waukesha, with one fatality, a female by the name of Elise Taggert. Her badly burned body was identified by the dog tattoo on her right ankle. Cause of the fire was a shorted out appliance in her apartment. That's impossible, Elise thought to herself. She could feel panic rising up in her whole body, like a giant wave on the ocean, ready to knock her off her feet. What was going on here? She heard footsteps coming down the hall and quickly closed the page she was looking at, and clicked on a weather icon just as Harold came into the room.

"I see you're feeling better, and starting to make your way around the house," he said as he gave the quick peck on the forehead that he seemed to like doing, "this is a lovely study, isn't it? I remember when we picked out this desk for you, at an estate auction. Remember that?"

"Not really, but yes, it is a beautiful room, and I do love the desk." She decided not to discuss her memories or anything else with Harold for now, until she could find out what was going on. Instead, she simply asked, "do you remember the password on my laptop?"

"Of course, it's our wedding anniversary, 20June06," he said with a smile, "coming up on our eighth anniversary very soon. Why do you suddenly need to use your laptop? Not the first thing I'd think you'd do as your memory improves."

"It's a good start. I must have photos, emails, files, and other things on here. They might help me remember me," she said innocently. "What do I do for a living? Do I have a job I need to get back to?"

"A job? No, I don't think so, Mel, I provide more than adequately for you, you don't need to work, and haven't since we got married. You tend to your gardens, go to your garden groups, decorate the house, and manage the help," he said with a rude snort of a laugh.

"Manage the help? You mean Marjorie? How much managing does she need? Do I plan the meals with her or what?" she asked, playing the role she'd been given.

"Marjorie quite capably plans the meals, but we also have Marie, our housekeeper, who is Marjorie's sister and Raphael, Marjorie's husband, who takes care of the yard, the gardens and pool," Harold told her impatiently. "One of these days you are going to have to try and remember some of this stuff yourself, you know."

"I'm trying Harold, this is all new to me," she said, not looking at him. "Think of it as if you're explaining everything to a stranger."

"Fine. I'm sorry, I'm trying to remember you aren't doing this on purpose," Harold sighed. "I need to get back to the office, I'll see you at dinner time. Have Marjorie or Marie spend some time with you this afternoon. They can explain the workings of the household better than I can, since you always took care of it."

"I'll do that, Harold," she said, returning her attention to the laptop. Without another word, he left the room.

Elise, for that was who she was certain she was, sat silently for a moment staring at the blank screen, pondering what her next move should be. If she wasn't Melody, which she was pretty sure she wasn't, then where was Melody? Perhaps she should call the police and report her missing? But call them and say what? There's a woman missing, who is my husband's real wife, only everyone is pretending I'm his wife, but I'm not? I'm the person who supposedly died in a fire a couple weeks ago….Okay, that's not going to work, she thought to herself, but then what? She wished she could remember everything from her past, but a lot of it was still fuzzy. She knew it would come back to her, but she wished it would hurry up. And was there even a slight chance that Harold was telling the truth? She really was Melody, and everything she was remembering were false memories from a jumbled brain? She really didn't think so, but could she be certain 100%? No. She needed someone to help her, and she didn't know who to trust, so the police were her only option. She looked up their number quickly, before she changed her mind, and dialed the phone.

"Delafield police department, Officer Martin speaking, can I help you?" came the crisp greeting almost immediately.

"Hello, could I talk to a policeman, about a possible missing person?" she hesitated, almost hanging up the phone mid-sentence.

"Did you need to file a missing person report? Is this an adult? How long have they been missing?" The man on the other end fired questions at her.

"I'm not sure, I just need to talk to someone, to see if they can help me," she said quietly.

"Ma'am, do you know if someone is actually missing?"

"Not exactly, it's all rather confusing. I was in an accident, and couldn't remember things, and now I'm starting to remember who I am, but the papers say I'm dead, but it's very confusing...." Elise was rambling and didn't know what to say. "I guess I shouldn't have called, I'm sorry for wasting.."

"Hold on, you need some help? Let me see if I can find someone to talk to you," Officer Martin replied in a kinder voice, "I'm going to put you on hold for a second and transfer you to someone who might be able to help you."

"All right, thank you," she replied quietly. She toyed with the idea of hanging up, but that would be really rude now that he was trying to find someone to talk to her, so she hung on. A second officer, by the name of Patricia Lang, came on the line and with a very kind sounding voice, asked a few questions and asked her to hold the line for a moment. She came back and explained that given the circumstances, and her muddled memory, it might be better if she talked off the record. She had a good friend, who happened to be a police man too, but also had a lot of connections that were useful for people in strange situations. He would be able to get her to someone who could definitely help her. Elise agreed to talk to him, if only because she had no other idea what to do. She waited on hold for a few more minutes, toying with hanging up the phone.

"Detective Scolari, homicide, what can I do for you?" came a new friendly voice.

"Homicide? Oh no, there's been a mistake, I don't have a homicide to report, I think I have a missing person to report. No one is dead....well, they say I am, but that isn't me. I'm not dead. But I think my husband's wife is missing. He's not really my husband, he just says he is....oh this is all coming out so complicated. I shouldn't have called." Elise babbled, unable to make any sense at all.

"Hold on a sec, slow down. Patty told me you have a complicated situation you need some help with. Suppose you tell me a few things, and I'll figure out what we need to do. Let's start with the easy stuff first, what's your name, ma'am?" Scolari said.

"Well, it's either Elise Taggert or Melody Richardson. It's complicated," she said with a deep sigh.

"Go ahead, I'm listening," he said kindly. Elise told him as clearly as she could about her predicament, trying to keep it as simple as possible. After a few minutes, she was finished, and told him she didn't know what to do, so she called the police.

"I don't think this is exactly a police matter, but you do obviously need some help getting things straightened out, and I know someone who can help you do that. He's a private investigator, not too far from you. I know him personally, and he's a real good guy. He can get to the bottom of this for you if anyone can. Reasonable priced too. I'll give you his number, his name is Zachary Marchand. I'll let him know to expect your call," Scolari told her, sounding very pleased with himself. "Trust me, you'll like Zach, and he will be able to help you get things straightened out ."

Elise thanked him, wrote down the number and hung up. She wasn't quite ready to make that call, but she knew she'd have to, sooner rather than later.

Chapter 4

Elise sat with the phone in her hand for a few minutes, then with a sigh, hung it up. Maybe she was being silly. Maybe she really was Melody and this was her home. Brain injuries can do strange things. She remembered seeing a show on TV where a woman woke up from a coma and suddenly spoke with a British accent the rest of her life.

She wandered around the house, looking in each expansive room, picking things up, looking out windows, hoping something would jar her memory even a little bit. But there was nothing. She wandered out into the garden. It was stunning, like a beautiful English rose garden, full of roses in all different colors and sizes. There were trellises for some to grow on, while others were hearty free standing bushes. An exquisite white gazebo stood in the center of the garden, with little benches inside, and stone paths leading off in several directions from it. It was peaceful out there and the scent of the roses was intoxicating. Elise sat down on a bench in the gazebo, trying to connect with the lovely place. But all it did was frustrate her further. If she belonged here, why couldn't she remember any of it? Why did she instead remember a cozy little apartment several miles away, with thrift store furnishings? And how could it be possible that apartment had burned, with a woman in it? A woman that was supposedly her? It was too confusing to think about. She went back inside and retreated to the ridiculously extravagant bedroom and crawled back into bed. In sleep she didn't have to wonder who she was or why she was here.

The next day, Harold coaxed her downstairs for breakfast, where Marjorie once again fussed over her like a protective mother. She efficiently served them their meals and retreated to the kitchen.

"How are you feeling today?" Harold asked.

"I'm feeling okay, but I'm still not remembering any of this," Elise said with a wave of her hand.

"What is it you are remembering? Your jeans and a little apartment again?" He asked with a laugh that fell a little short of kindly.

"Yes, in fact, I can remember all of that pretty clearly. Not everything, but enough to know I don't belong here," Elise said, needing to see his reaction.

"Well, enjoy your little delusions if you must, but in time you will come to accept this as your home and your life," he said with a deep sigh as he sat back in his chair. "There are worse things than having this as your life, don't you think? Even if you had a pathetic life in a dingy little apartment previously, wouldn't it be nice to trade up to this life?"

"What are you saying? Trading up to this life? This isn't my life. I'm not your wife. Don't you get that?" Elise asked, becoming angered by his comments.

"Calm down, all I'm saying is if you think you remember that other life as real, think of this as a great new life you've traded the old one in for. Most people would be thrilled at an opportunity like that. To be able to leave a struggling, pauper's existence, and live here instead. No need to work, all your worries taken care of. Kind of like winning the lottery," he said with a smug smile.

"I guess that would be great if a person had a miserable life and wanted to trade it for something like this. I didn't, and I don't. You can't keep me here and force me to be your wife, you know," Elise said, staring intently at him.

"Of course not! You've never been a prisoner here. You are free to go any time you want to. But you've lived here for almost eight years, Melody. Where will you go? The Elise Taggert you claim to be died in a fire in her apartment. You can't go live there. What are you going to do?" He said, returning her intense stare. "Leave right now if you feel you must, or give yourself some time to come to your senses."

Elise looked away from him and stared out the nearby window. What would she do? Where would she go. She had to figure something out before just walking out the door. "I will try it for a few days, but I think you're badly mistaken. I'm reasonably sure I am not your Melody."

For the next two days, Elise tried her best to feel at home in the luxurious house, but it didn't happen. Even with the friendly Marjorie and Marie trying their best to jog her memory, Elise knew this wasn't her home. The comments Harold had made over breakfast, about trading her old life for this fancy new one, bothered her the more she thought about it. Was he up to something? Was he really trying to get her to trade her old life to live here as his wife? She wasn't sure of much, and her mind was still cloudy, but she somehow knew she couldn't trust Harold. She needed to talk to someone she could trust. She went back into the fancy study and rummaged around for a piece of paper where she had written a phone number down a few days ago. It was time to make that phone call, and hopefully take the first step to getting her life back.

*   *   *   *   *

Zachary Marchand was trying to clean off his desk, have lunch and answer a few emails, all at the same time. His desk had a way of becoming buried by papers, files, envelopes, assorted post-it notes, pens and pencils, so he was forced to perch his tuna salad on rye on top of the mess. He made a feeble attempt to rein in the clutter, but the chaos was always a few steps ahead of him. And why, if there were tablets and pens scattered all over the place, did they always disappear the minute he needed to write something down? Kelly was his secretary, receptionist and go to assistant for just about everything. She cleaned up in here occasionally, but mostly it was his domain. He finished his sandwich, gulped down the last of his lime Diet Coke, and tossed the lunch wrappings in the general direction of the trash can on the opposite side of the room. Missing the can as usual, he sighed, got up, and dropped the trash into the can.

"No quitting my day job for a career in basketball, I guess," he shrugged. He ran his fingers through his unruly thick sandy brown hair, a headful that most women would kill for, grabbed his jacket and headed for the door. He got as far as touching the doorknob when Kelly called him back.

"Mr. Marchand, here's a call I think you need to take, I'm not making any bets on it," Kelly said as she motioned to the phone, "but this might be the one your detective friend told you about a few days ago."

Zach turned around, raised his eyebrows, and came back for the call.

"Hello, this is Zachary Marchand, how can I help you?" he said, using his most professional voice.

"Mr. Marchand, a police detective gave me your name and said you might be able to help me," came a very scared voice on the other end. "I'm not sure anyone can figure out this mess I'm in the middle of, but I've been told you are my best hope."

"Well, that's quite an endorsement, I'll try my best. Would you like to stop by so we can discuss your dilemma?" Zach asked.

"I can't drive yet. I was in an accident and I'm not thinking too clearly yet. I could take a cab to you," Elise said, unsure of how to proceed.

"Or I can come to you if that would be easier," Zach offered, knowing that frequently people seemed to open up more in their own homes than in his office.

"That would be wonderful. If you can come when my husband, uh, Harold, isn't here. Let me find you the address," she left the phone for a minute or two, and came back with the information for Zach, "he will be gone until dinner if you can come this afternoon."

"I can do that, I'll see you around two, would that be okay?" Zach said as he wrote down her information. "And what did you say your name was?"

"Oh, my name. Yes, well it's either Elise Taggert I'm pretty sure, or maybe Melody Richardson. Thank you very much for helping me, Mr. Marchand."

Zach hung up the phone and turned to Kelly with a smile. "That was the call we've been warned about. I'm going to see her at two today. She's right in Delafield. Can you see what you can find out about either name before I go?" He gave both names to Kelly, the wheels already turning in his mind. As he left to attend to earlier business, he wondered why this woman didn't know who she was, and why she had to go look up her own address.

Zach drove to Franklin, one of the newer suburbs to grow out of Milwaukee. It was a bustling area, with a lot of large condo communities. He was headed to one of these condos to meet with Alvin Hooper, who was sure someone was tampering with the sliding doors on his balcony, trying to get in. Police were unable to help him, so he called Zach to find out who it was and what they were trying to do.

Alvin, a short balding man with a severe comb-over and a bottle of beer in his chubby fist, was waiting for him on his porch as Zach drove up in his shiny new red Chevy Colorado pickup truck. He instructed Rudy, his attentive new canine sidekick, to stay in the truck. Rudy had been a gift to a client who was having a very rough time when her children had been abducted. Once she got her children back, and her life got back to normal, she didn't feel it was fair to the puppy to be kenneled all day while she worked, so she had reluctantly given the dog back to Zach. She did insist on visitation rights, and the two of them had become good friends. As it turned out, Rudy was just what a dateless Zach needed for company. The stocky little German Shepherd was smart as a whip and cuddly as hell. Zach already adored the not-so-little guy.

Zach met Alvin on his porch as Alvin immediately began a tirade about someone trying to break into his condo by way of his sliding doors on his balcony.

"I've seen evidence of at least three attempts over the last few weeks, and the police ain't interested," Alvin sputtered as he walked Zach through the condo to the sliding doors off the living room.

Zach let Alvin finish spouting off all his anger before he started questioning him. "Exactly what evidence did you find? Are there pry marks on the doors, broken glass?"

"Nah, nah, nothing like that. Nothin' that obvious," Alvin said, shaking his head and waving his hands all at once. "First time I noticed, was a couple, three weeks ago, when we had that last little snowfall, ya know? Just enough of a covering so I could see two hand sized spots missing on the railing out there. And then I noticed some big oval spots, coulda been foot prints, right on the balcony, less than two feet from the door!"

"Were they footprints, do you think? Did they actually look like foot prints? Or hand prints on the railing?" Zach asked, trying to get an idea what the guy had actually seen. "You didn't happen to take any pictures of them, did you?"

"Nah, I should have. I called the police and they sent a guy over, in no big hurry I might add, and he had a look for himself, but he said they were just bare spots, and didn't look like anything. Said the door didn't look disturbed, so there wasn't anything they could do. Does some crook actually have to bust in here and take everything I own before the cops can do anything?" Alvin started another tirade, and Zach cut him off before he got going full speed.

"That would not be good, Mr. Hooper, you said there were other times, more recent. Can you tell me about them?" Zach asked, jotting down a few things in the little notebook he kept in his pocket. They were standing on the balcony now, and it didn't look too inviting to him. There were several old clay pots standing at one end, with what looked liked the remnants of plants that had died over winter. Two old wrought iron cafe chairs, were sitting next to the plants, along with a small round matching table. The whole balcony looked badly in need of some paint, as did the furniture.

One of the chairs had been tipped forward onto the table, and the clay pot next to it was lying on it's side, cracked, with the contents spilling out.

"Ok, last week Tuesday, I come home from work, and one of my patio chairs here was knocked over! The wind don't knock 'em over, I keep 'em in the corner like, it's protected there. And they're metal! Have to be a hell of a wind to come around a corner and knock over a steel chair. It had to be kicked over or something. And there was a little dirt on the floor here. Probably from a guy's shoe." Seeing a doubtful look come across Zach's face, Alvin hurriedly continued, "then, yesterday, I come home, I come in, toss my jacket on the couch over there, and outta the corner of my eye, I can see something moving on the balcony! The blinds were drawn, but I could still make out something dark, move across the balcony and jump over the railing! By the time I got the darn door open and got out there, ain't no one there. But sure enough, more dirt on the floor, one of my plants knocked over, and the chair tipped over again. I left everything just like I found it this time, just so's you could see for yourself. I'm off work today, using my day off to meet you here and keep an eye on things!"

"Mr. Hooper, I don't see any sign of an attempted break in. No marks on the door jamb, nothing like that. Maybe it's a neighbor kid messing with you?" Zach suggested.

"Well maybe, but I don't know! That's why I hired you, you guys do stuff like this. I don't have no grudges with any neighbors, so I don't know who would do this. I'm hoping you can get to the bottom of it." Alvin polished off the last of his beer and wiped his mouth on his sleeve.

"All right Mr. Hooper, I think I have enough information. I'll see what I can find out. I'm pretty sure we can find an answer for you. I'm going to have a look around downstairs, below your balcony, before I leave. I'll be in touch," Zach said as he walked back through the cramped condo and down to the side yard.

"Thanks a lot, I knew I could count on you," Alvin called to him as he closed his door.

Zach walked around under the balcony, looking for anything that might look out of place. The ground was pretty thawed by now, but not so soft that footprints were evident. Besides, it was mostly grass. While some of it was somewhat flattened, it didn't indicate anything. Zach decided to come back tomorrow, in the middle of the day when the disturbances seemed to be taking place. He'd make sure Mr. Hooper would be going to work as usual. He hopped back into his truck where Rudy was waiting for a good neck rub, and they drove off. Time for a trip to Delafield.

The address on Millridge Road in Delafield took Zach to a stunning brick home surrounded by a beautiful flower garden. He gave a low whistle as he pulled up in the circular drive. "No peeing in their yard, Rudy," he said with a smile as he left the pup in the driver's seat.

Zach was greeted by a friendly woman, who introduced herself as Marie, the housekeeper. She guided him to the side garden, where Elise was waiting for him.

"Thank you so much for coming, Mr. Marchand, I'm kind of a prisoner here, with this darn broken foot, and my messed up head," Elise said with a weak laugh as she invited him to sit down.

"Beautiful place you have here, taking care of all the gardens looks like a full time," Zach said warmly as he shook her hand and sat.

"Yes, it is, there's a man who tends the gardens and the pool," she said, unsure of how to proceed. She needn't have worried, for

Zach took over quickly.

"First of all, what would you like me to call you? Elise, Melody, Mrs. Taggert…" he began.

"Please, just Elise, for now anyway. This is all going to sound very complicated, so please bear with me. I don't know all the details myself yet, I'm still remembering more every day. I had some sort of amnesia from the accident, and things are still a little mixed up." She gave a slow sigh and continued, "let me start at the beginning."

For the next hour, Elise told Zach about waking up in the strange bedroom in this beautiful, but strange house, next to a strange man who claimed to be her husband. She told him all the details about not remembering any of the house or the people associated with it, even though they all seemed to know her. She told him about remembering who she thought she really was, about her apartment and her life. She explained how Harold had told her these memories were false and the real ones would emerge in time. Zach didn't say anything as she spoke, though he did record the whole thing so he could listen to it again later. She finished by telling him about the reports she read online, where a woman died in an apartment fire, and she was identified as Elise Taggert by the dog tattoo on her ankle. She sat back, took a long drink of water, closed her eyes and spoke softly.

"And that's when I called you, Mr. Marchand, what on earth do I do now?"

Chapter 5

"Well! That's a heck of a story, Elise," Zach said as he expelled the breath he had been holding, "I guess to start with, we need to find out if you really are Elise Taggert. Once we know that for sure, we can work from there. So as you're remembering things, nothing in this house is even remotely familiar? Except maybe Harold?"

"Right, him just a little bit, but nothing else. Even the clothes in my...the closet, that's not the sort of things I wear, I know that. I wear jeans, and there isn't a single pair to be found in this house. Harold said I've never owned a pair. Maybe Melody didn't, but I'm sure I did!" Elise said, becoming animated as she spoke.

"Alright, I'm going to do some digging, look into the woman that died in that fire, check around that neighborhood, talk to some of the people who might have been in contact with you regularly. I'm going to take a couple photos of you, to show them, okay?" Zach explained as he pulled out his smart phone and took a few head shots of Elise. "You just sit tight until I get back to you, which I'll do as soon as I can."

"Please don't call the house, Harold might answer and I don't want to tell him I'm doing this. I don't know what to think of him yet, but I don't think I totally trust him," Elise said with a bit of panic evident in her voice.

"No, I won't, I already thought of that," he said as he fished a disposable cell phone out of his pocket and handed it to her. "Use this to call me, and I'll use it to contact you. You can silence the ringer, but check it frequently, all right? Do you feel safe here, or do you want me to take you somewhere else?"

"No, I'll just play along, as the wife with no memory. I'll be fine here, Marjorie is very sweet, and so is Marie. But thank you. I don't feel quite so alone and helpless now. Please find out something fast." Elise said with a small smile, "I'm not sure how long I can play the part of a pampered, rich wife."

Before Zach drove off, he made a quick call to Kelly, so by the time he got to the office, she had plenty to fill him in on.

"Okay, this looks like it's going to be interesting," Kelly greeted him as he and Rudy arrived. Rudy took up his spot next to Zach's desk, found his bone from that morning and resumed work on it. "First of all, what was she like? Does she really not know who she is?"

"I think she's pretty sure who she is, but she needs some sort of proof, since everything right now is pointing to her being someone else," Zach smiled and looked over her shoulder at the first of several sites she had open on her computer. "What do we have here?"

"This is the police report of the fire in that apartment in Waukesha. It says the victim was the woman who lived there, by the name of Elise Taggert, single female, caucasian, thirty four years old. Her body was badly burned, and she was identified mainly by the tattoo on her right ankle. The coroner said her size, age and hair color all fit. Cause of death was undetermined, but assumed to be smoke inhalation," Kelly read, "the odd thing that stands out is the fact that only her apartment went up in flames. None of the adjoining ones had much damage at all. They think some small appliance shorted out, but were unable to identify anything for sure."

"Interesting. So as far as the world is concerned, Elise Taggert is dead. What else you got?" he asked as he ran his fingers though his hair.

"Next, the report of the accident involving Melody Richardson. She was westbound on highway 18, when a pickup truck ran a stop sign at Gramling Lane and t-boned her. She suffered a broken nose, fractured cheekbone, severe lacerations on her forehead, broken right foot and severe concussion. She was taken to Summit Medical Center, then almost immediately transferred at her husband's request to a small, unnamed private hospital in Oconomowoc. The driver of the pickup truck was cited. He had only minor injuries. He's the one who immediately called the police when he hit her. Her husband said she was on her way to their cabin for the weekend, and the luggage she had with her supports that." Kelly continued to explain her findings to Zach even though he was reading over her shoulder. It helped him think.

"Ok, all of this seems pretty straightforward. Elise died in an apartment fire and Melody was in an accident. So why does the woman I met today think she's Elise, but living Melody's life? She has the injuries that Melody received, she even remembers the accident and being put in an ambulance," Zach said, rubbing his face with his hand, "so why doesn't it all add up?"

"Who says it doesn't? Maybe her husband is right, she's just having mixed up memories, and she really is Melody." Kelly suggested, "it's the simplest solution. You know what they say, if it looks like a duck, and quacks like a duck…."

"I know, but some of the things she said, little things, like she remembers her apartment and the neighborhood, and that she always wore jeans, and not much else. In this place she's living now, there isn't a pair of jeans in the house. And she remembers nothing of the house, the people there, nothing. Don't you think if she's starting to remember things, some of the most basic things in her life would come back?" Zach said, questioning himself as much as Kelly, "and why would she be remembering herself as a woman who conveniently died in a fire the same day of her accident. Something isn't right here. It's almost as if the two women's minds were switched, which is impossible."

"That would be one for the books," Kelly said, furrowing her brow, then added, "here's a simple question, which one does she look like?"

"Another problem. These two women look similar enough to be twins. They're only a few years apart in age, but same build, same hair color and almost the same hair style. Same eye color, and if we had a stack of photos of each of them and mixed them up, we'd have a hard time telling them apart." Zach sounded understandably frustrated. "Getting fingerprints or dental records for her might be handy, except most likely she's never been fingerprinted, and she has no idea who her dentist is, as either woman."

"So what are you going to do? Where to start?" Kelly asked.

"Great question, kiddo," Zach said, shaking his head. "Guess I'll start with this Harold guy, who claims to be her husband."

Zach spent the next few hours looking up everything he could find about Harold Richardson. And he found a lot. Harold was a successful criminal lawyer, a decent looking guy in his early forties, who seemed to have a lot of interesting connections, and enjoyed a busy social life. His picture was all over the place at social events, fund raisers, dinners, whatever. Sometimes his wife was with him and sometimes not. Melody was his second wife. He had two children with his first wife, but no mention of any involvement with them beyond the divorce announcement and custody settlement. Harold's father, Ernest Richardson II, was an incredibly wealthy and successful attorney, and senior partner at his own law firm. This was the same firm where Harold worked. Ernest kept a tight rein on his whole family. Besides Harold, the eldest, he had two other sons, Thomas and Edward, and a daughter Virginia. Though all adults, he still called the shots for how they lived their lives, ran their careers and handled their families. He forever dangled their generous monthly stipends and a massive inheritance in front of them like a carrot on a stick. Ernest had no patience for one of his children not being able to take proper care of their family. Harold was already on thin ice for having divorced his first wife, the mother of his two children. Fortunately those children were both girls, and not in line to become Ernest Richardson the third. Once Harold remarried, Ernest held out hope for a grandson to carry on his name. Harold knew that having a son would give him the brunt of his father's massive fortune, and he'd like nothing better than to get his hands on all that money. So far, in eight years, that hadn't happened. But they were still apparently happily married, so for now, Ernest was appeased. A second divorce and Harold knew he'd be written out of any inheritance completely. Harold wasn't about to let that happen.

"Ok, so the Richardsons are one tightly knit family, whether they like it or not," Zach mused out loud, "and old dad holds the purse strings pretty tightly. Not sure if that's relevant, seeing that Harold must make a decent living even without dad's money." After reading all he could find on Harold, it was time to check out Elise Taggert's stomping grounds.

Zach piled Rudy into his truck and headed to Buckley Street in Waukesha. Figuring more people would be around in the evening, he parked near the apartment complex and had a look around. There were a good number of apartment buildings in the area, a couple of large churches, a convenience store, a thrift shop and a gas station. No friendly little corner bistro where Elise might have stopped in every day, where the owners would know her. The downtown area was about two blocks away. He sighed and decided to have a look inside the building before venturing down there.

Elise had lived, and supposedly died, on the 4th floor, apartment 418. He took the elevator to the 4th floor, noting the lobby entrance wasn't even locked. Apartment 418 and the ones on either side of it, 416 and 420, had their doors wide open and a lot of work was going on inside. He poked his head inside 416.

"Hey, fellas? Anyone here know the lady who died in the fire?" Zach called to the men laying carpeting.

"Nah, we just do work for the complex. That's over 300 apartments, man, don't get too familiar with any of the folks," a young man in a muscle shirt said, not looking up from his work. "You could ask Paulie though, in the next apartment, he's like an old wash woman, he knows everybody!" He laughed, and so did the other three guys in the room.

Zach walked over to 418. It was hard to believe this was an apartment that had been pretty much gutted by fire less than two weeks ago. The drywall and framing had already been replaced, new woodwork, new carpet all in, and kitchen cabinets were going up right now.

"Paulie in here?" Zach called as he entered the little unit.

"Who wants to know?" A burly guy with colorful tattoos up and down both arms asked as he hoisted a cabinet onto the wall.

"Name's Zach, private investigator. Looking for anyone who knew the lady who died here. I was told you might know her," Zach said hopefully.

"Barely knew her, enough to say hi to her in the hall, but not like I'd recognize her if I saw her on the street," he shook his head, keeping his eyes on the guy screwing in the cabinet he was holding up. Then he nodded his head to the side. "Try 408, I think they were friends."

"Thanks, I'll do that," Zach said as he left. A knock on the door of 408 created a ton of annoying high pitched yipping and barking, followed by an almost as high pitched warning for them to knock it off. A minute later, the door opened and Zach was staring at a tall, thin, youngish man, loaded with earrings and various other facial piercings. His lips were black and his blonde hair hung almost to his waist. He was wearing skinny black jeans and a tight long sleeve tee with wide black and white stripes. He had two tiny terriers in his arms, one wearing a pink polka dotted shirt and the other a bright green skirt with stars on it. They had ribbons on the tops of their heads to match their outfits. A third Yorkie frantically circled his feet, trying to jump into his arms. This one was dressed in purple. For a second, Zach was without words.

"Ahhh, hi! Name's Zach. I'm looking for anyone who knew the lady who died in the fire," he said as he motioned to the burned out apartment.

"Oh my God can you believe that? Poor Elise! I still can't believe she's gone!" the man gasped, clutching his little dogs closer to his boney chest. "Are you a friend of hers? I don't recall ever meeting you before."

"No, I'm not, I'm a private investigator, looking into a personal matter, and I need to get some details on Elise's life, and her death." Zach said honestly, without divulging anything.

"It was so sad! I saw her the night before. We had some wine together and she was showing me some things I could do to tame these little creatures, but wait, please, come in, come in," he motioned with a wide sweep of his hand.

Zach wasn't sure what he was expecting, but the interior of the apartment was a surprise. There were several huge circus posters on the available wall space, but all the furnishings were stark, simple pieces in black and white. All the accent pieces and knick-knacks were circus themed, and colorful as well. It was an interesting look. "Neat looking place you have here," he had to say.

"Thank you, I decorated it myself. And I am a professional clown, can you believe that?" he giggled.

"That's pretty cool, never met a professional clown before," Zach smiled.

"So what can I tell you about Elise? Would you like a beer or a wine cooler? My name is Bastian, by the way, I'm pleased to meet you!" He ran off and returned with two bottles of beer before Zach could answer him, and handed Zach a Samuel Adams Winter Lager. Bastian had good taste in beers.

"How well did you know Elise? Were you good friends?" Zach asked as he pulled several photos from his pocket and handed them to Bastian.

"Yes, yes, we were great friends! I think she was my BFF, you know? I miss her terribly. She didn't judge people by their looks, she looked deeper. Great lady. We touched bases at least a few times a week, had dinner together couple times a month," Bastian said as he took the photos and studied them. Zach had handed him a few each of Elise and Melody.

"Well now this is curious, are these supposed to be Elise? I don't think so. This one here, I think this is Elise, but her nose looks wrong, and her eyes aren't quite right, and her hair was longer. Wait, she's bruised in this photo, was she beaten or what?" Bastian babbled endlessly as he shuffled through the photos. "And this one, no this isn't her. There's a cold look in this woman's eyes, That is definitely not Elise."

"Thanks, that's very helpful. No she wasn't beaten, she was in a car accident. And you're probably right, the other photo you picked isn't Elise." Zach took the photos back.

"When was that photo taken? I don't remember her being in an accident, and that looks like a pretty recent photo," Bastian observed, "what's going on here, anyway?"

"That's what I'm trying to figure out," Zach said, "do you happen to know who helped the police identify her body? They mainly relied on a tattoo on her leg?"

"Yes! That was me! I went with her when she got that tat, she was too nervous to go into a tattoo parlor alone. Some weird people hang out in some of them, you know what I mean?" Bastian explained as he put the dogs on the floor. "It was definitely her tattoo, look, I got the same one, that same day, so she wasn't so nervous about it! She watched me get mine first!" He pushed up the tight fabric of his jeans to reveal a tattoo of an Irish wolfhound on his ankle. "Kind of looks like a giant version of one of my little sweeties," he laughed.

"Well, I'm guessing there aren't a lot of people with that same tattoo, in that same place on their leg," Zach sighed. "So it was Elise that died in that fire, no doubt in your mind?"

"Unfortunately no. She was horribly burned, but the tattoo

was quite visible, sort of raised even. I guess the heat of the fire did that. And you could tell she had jeans on, there was enough of her clothing to see that. Elise lived in jeans. I don't think I've ever seen her in a dress," Bastian said sadly, remembering his good friend.

"Do you know why they didn't check her dental records to verify it was her?" Zach asked, curious.

"Well, I think there wasn't any question about it being her or not, and her dentist's name would have been in her address book or her phone, both of which went up in flames with everything else."

"Well, I appreciate your time, you've been really helpful, thanks a lot." Zack said as he rose to go.

"Anytime, I enjoyed our visit," Bastian said with a smile, "but you still didn't tell me when you got the picture of Elise with the bruises."

"That's a real funny thing," Zach said thoughtfully, "I took those this afternoon."

Chapter 6

"What?? She's alive? Elise is alive?" Bastian gasped as he fell back into his chair, "but how can that be possible? I saw her. She was very, very dead. I went to her funeral, for God's sake!" All the color drained from his face as his arms fell to his sides.

"It's very complicated, and I don't know how much I should say at this time," Zach spoke seriously, "can I count on you to keep this a little quiet for now? I'm not sure I want a lot of people knowing about this."

"Of course! Of Course, I won't breathe a word to a soul! Is she alive? Tell me!"

"I think so. At least I'm pretty sure she is. She's my client, and she thinks she is Elise, but she can't remember a whole lot of her past right now. She was in an accident the same night as the apartment fire, and the man she's living with claims she's his wife. Named Melody. That's the other woman in the pictures I showed you. Elise is starting to remember bits of her past, like the fact that she wore jeans all the time, but not a whole lot more than that yet. Zach proceeded to give Bastian the Reader's Digest version of everything that was going on, in hopes that he might think of something Zach had overlooked. He did.

"Maybe if I go see her, she'll remember me?" Bastian suggested. "I can't go tonight as I'm due on stage in an hour or so, but what about tomorrow? Where is she anyway?"

"That might be a great help. If she remembers you, she has to be Elise, doesn't she? Why didn't I think of that, I do this stuff for a living!" Zach joked. "Give me a call tomorrow and we can figure out when we can get the two of you together."

As Zach made the drive back home, with Rudy sleeping soundly next to him, he was pretty pleased with himself. He had lucked out and hooked up with Bastian instead of wasting endless hours poking around the neighborhood asking about Elise. Having Bastian meet Elise would a giant first step towards solving this mystery. He pulled into an Arby's drive-thru, got a couple of roast beef sandwiches and went home to figure out his next moves. Rudy happily shared the sandwiches with him.

By morning, Zach was anxious to get going on Elise's cause. He really wanted to talk to some of the people in Harold's house but wasn't sure how to do that without alerting Harold. He texted Elise to see if she was available, and she was. Harold wouldn't be home until late, so they had the whole day. He questioned Elise a little about the hired help, and thought maybe Marjorie or her sister Marie might talk to him. He decided to take a chance, and headed over there.

Marie met him at the door almost as soon as he knocked. "May I help you?" the handsome Hispanic woman asked.

"Hello ma'am, I met you yesterday, Marie, isn't it?" Zach flashed his best smile.

"I am indeed, and who did you say you were?" she replied, one hand immediately going to her chest.

"My name is Zach ma'am. I'm a friend of…Melody's, and I'm trying to help her with her memory lapses. May I talk to you and your sister for a moment? I won't take a lot of your time," he said, pouring on the charm.

"Please! Of course, come in, we can talk in the kitchen. Marjorie is in there baking up something, we can talk while she works. This way please," she welcomed him inside and bustled quickly down a long hall, past several elegant rooms and into a spacious, chef quality kitchen.

"Shall I get Mrs. Richardson to join us?" Marie asked as she directed Zach to a chair at the large wooden table. A second woman, who had to be Marjorie, brushed some flour from her hands, and immediately set a cup of coffee and a platter of fresh pastries in front of him.

"No, let's not get her just yet. I'd like to spend a few minutes with the two of you first," he said, almost salivating at the sight of the bakery in front of him. "This isn't necessary, Marjorie, you are Marjorie, am I right?"

"I am indeed, and I consider it an insult for anyone to come into my kitchen before ten o'clock and not have a couple of my home made pastries," she said with a smile as she set a plate and napkins in front of him.

"Well! In that case, I certainly don't want to offend anyone," Zach smiled at her as he selected a yummy looking filled pastry. It was still warm.

"That's better, now how can we help you help Melody?" Marjorie said as she joined them at the table.

"As you both know, she's having a hard time remembering things. She needs to get her memory back and get on with her life, don't you agree?" Zach asked, wanting to feel them out a bit.

"Of course she needs to. She is very nice to us, but she acts like she doesn't know us," Marjorie said sadly, then added, "but she's very sweet, even so."

"Do you notice anything different about her since she's come home? Anything at all?" Zack asked.

"Well, she does seem nicer, more patient, but I attribute that to her not knowing how things run here, so she has to ask us for help," Marie said thoughtfully.

"That's right she is, but it's more than not knowing things," Marjorie agreed, then added, "she seems like she enjoys talking to us, you know, as people, not just hired help."

"She wasn't like that before the accident?" Zack asked. "How was she?"

"No, not really. She was polite and pleasant, but not friendly. Didn't talk to us any more than necessary," Marie explained, thinking about her answer.

"Yes, that's it! She talks to us now because she wants to, not because she needs to," Marjorie nodded her head. "Do you think the bump on her head did that?"

"I don't know about that, but it is interesting," Zack agreed, then decided to push his luck a bit. "What about physically? Does she still look like the same woman?"

"Well, no matter how badly she hit her head, she's still the same woman," Marjorie scoffed, "even if she doesn't look quite the same."

"No, Marjorie, you know we talked about this, let's tell this nice gentleman what we were saying." Marie coaxed her sister. "No one else is listening to us, maybe he will."

"If the mister ever found out we did, we'd both be without jobs or a home!" Marjorie blurted out in a huff, visibly upset.

"Ladies, please. I promise you, nothing you tell me will get back to Mr. Richardson or anyone else. I'm just trying to get Melody's life straightened out for her," Zach reassured both of them, wondering what they didn't want to discuss.

"Alright, but we never told you this," Marjorie said. She seemed partly reluctant to talk and partly dying to tell someone. "She's changed. It's no big thing, but a lot of little things. Like talking to us as if we were equals. Coming into the kitchen to have a cup of coffee with me when I take a break. Asking me to get something for the kitchen, instead of telling me to get it. Just small things like that. At first I thought the bang on the head just mellowed her out. But then I noticed she looks younger than before. Not a lot, more like a very refreshed version of herself. Of course she's still a bit bruised and swollen, but she still looks fresher."

"Some of her mannerisms have changed too," Marie added, patting her sister's hand as she spoke. "The way she walks, the way she picks things up, all seem a little different. I know she has that cast on her foot, but she still walks like she has a purpose, not just gliding about like before. And her face is different. I know she needed to have some work done to fix her nose and all, but should that change her whole face? Sometimes I look at her and I think I don't know her at all."

Zach took a deep breath, looked from one woman to the other, then spoke. "You've confided in me all your concerns. Now can I tell you something that cannot leave this room?"

"Oh goodness yes! We won't breath a word to a soul!" Marjorie gushed as Marie nodded her head vigorously.

"I don't think Melody is Melody. I mean, the woman living here, is not the Melody you knew. The woman here I'm pretty sure, is someone else entirely. What I don't know is how she ended up here and why Mr. Richardson insists she is his wife." Zach spoke softly, looking to see their reactions.

"I knew it! I told Marjorie yesterday that the missus was too nice to be the missus! I said someone switched her!" Marie jumped to her feet and burst out, then immediately sat back down.

"Good lord, what is going on here?" Marjorie asked, "if she isn't the missus, who is she? And where is the real one?"

"Those are two very good questions, and that's what I've been hired to find out," Zach started to explain.

"Hired? Who hired you? What are you? I thought you were a friend of the missus?" Marie ask, startled by his comment.

"I'm a private investigator, hired by her, though we think her name is Elise, not Melody. She's getting back bits of her memory, but instead of remembering this house and this life, she's remembering a totally different life, where she lived in an apartment in Waukesha." Zach explained calmly, putting them more at ease once again. "When she mentioned some of these memories to Harold, he told her they were false memories, not her real ones. Just some jumbled garbage from her confused mind. But the more she remembers, the more she thinks she is this other woman. So she called me to help her get to the bottom of all of it."

"Oh doesn't that beat all? Poor dear, doesn't know who she is or where she belongs, bless her heart." Marjorie wrung her chubby little hands together, "we will help any way we can, and you have our word, we won't breathe a word to anyone."

Zach then told them about meeting Bastian, and wanting to bring him to meet her, to see if she'd remember him.

"Bring him by, and we can say he's a nephew of ours, and we'd like her to meet him," Marie suggested.

"That's a great idea, Marie, I like that. I'll get a hold of him and see how soon he can come. Hopefully today yet." Zach nodded his head vigorously. "I'll visit a bit with Elise, before I go, and I'll get back to you as soon as I set something up with Bastian. You two have been a great help and I can't thank you enough."

Marie hurried off to fetch Elise and Marjorie took Zach, a pot of coffee and a platter of bakery out to the sunroom. "You can visit in here," she said with a smile, "this is so exciting, being part of a real mystery!"

Elise arrived a few minutes later. She looked stronger than when he saw her the first time.

"You're looking better, how is it going here?" he asked.

"It's going fine. As long as I keep up the forgetful wife act, Harold leaves me alone. And, he isn't around that much actually. Leaves pretty early and barely makes it home in time for dinner. But this is not my life. I'm sure of it. Have you learned anything yet? Is that why you've come?" Elise asked as she munched a bit of pastry.

"I've been doing a lot of digging, but nothing solid yet. I talked to Marjorie and Marie a bit, they're both very fond of you, you know." Zach said, wishing there was some way to pull the memories from her mind for her.

"They're both very sweet ladies. Melody had a nice life here it seems. But it's not for me. I don't want servants and hired people to do my work for me. I can cook and clean and shop, I'm not cut out for a pampered life like this. Seems like it would weaken a person, know what I mean?" Elise said softly.

"I think I do. Are you remembering anything more?"

"I keep remembering something about dogs. Did I have dogs? Worked with them maybe? I don't know. I hope I didn't have any that died in that fire! Did I?" she asked, bothered by the disturbing thought.

"I don't think so, there was no mention in the police report of any animals dying in the fire," Zach reassured her. "Remembering anything else? Other people who might remember you? Anything like that?"

"Not really, I tried to picture where I lived, but beyond it being an apartment, nothing. I must have had neighbors who knew me though," she rubbed her temples as if to squeeze a memory forward.

"I'm working on that. I'll be getting some answers for you very soon, don't worry," Zach reassured her. "I'll be back later today or tomorrow."

Zach said his goodbyes and called Bastian, leaving a message for him. Then he headed back to Franklin to do some sleuthing around a condo. He parked a few buildings away from Alvin Hooper's place, where he had a clear view of his balcony. He took out his binoculars and his lunch and sat back and got comfy. The balcony remained empty and undisturbed. Zach called into his office and got updates on several matters from Kelly, and more urgently, a message from Bastian. He would be happy to meet up with Zach that afternoon. Zach watched the balcony for another hour, then called it quits for the day. He was going to have to come up with something better than sitting here for a couple hours each day. He decided to try something else, and made a stop at Cabela's, an outdoor equipment store, then headed to his office, in the older section of the city of Brookfield.

His office was in one of the original buildings on the main street in Brookfield, aptly named Brookfield Road. The buildings were all frame structures with long porches and railings. Small signs stood in front of some of the shops, and awnings shaded their front windows. His office was on the south-west corner of the building, next to a small deli. There was also an insurance agency and a barber shop in the building, all in a row. It looked somewhat like it belonged in a Norman Rockwell painting. Small apartments were above the commercial buildings. The train tracks ran across the street, not more than a hundred feet from Zach's office. He loved the sound of train whistles as a kid, and that love had never diminished over the years. It was part of the reason he chose this building as his office location. That, and the low rent. Having lots of parking behind the building was nice too, along with a huge empty lot where he could play catch with Rudy. He pulled into a spot and went inside, ready to fill Kelly in on things and tell her Bastian was on his way. He didn't have to bother.

"Bastian, you got here already! That was fast," Zach greeted him warmly. "I see you've met my right hand girl."

"Zach, good to see you, yes, Kelly and I have been having a great visit," Bastian smiled. His outfit was decidedly different from what he had on yesterday, but just as unique. He had on plaid olive green parachute pants, a white boatneck tee shirt and a long, thin, colorful knit scarf wrapped around his neck several times. His long hair was in a single braid, and all his piercings were in place. "I rode my bike here, first day it's been warm enough to get it out."

Leaving Rudy to keep Kelly company, the two men hopped in Zach's truck and headed for Delafield. On the way, Zach filled Bastian in on what he had told Marjorie and Marie, and what they had told him. He informed Bastian that he was their visiting nephew.

As they arrived, Marie greeted them warmly at the front door. "Come in, come in, both of you! Into the kitchen, it's the friendliest room in the house!" She never even batted an eye at Bastian's appearance, which impressed Zach to no end.

Marjorie was waiting with coffee, fresh cinnamon pecan coffee cake and ice cream. "Sit down, young men," she greeted them as if they were all good friends. "And this must be our nephew, Bastian, is it? How good to meet you. I hope you don't mind me saying so, but you're a very colorful fellow! I didn't know we had anyone so colorful in our family! And you don't even look Hispanic!!" She laughed heartily at her own jokes, then brought over cups and condiments.

Marie returned a few moments later, with Elise in tow. It was all Bastian could do not to jump up and hug her since he thought she had died and had already attended her funeral. He barely managed to sit calmly and stir his coffee.

"Ma'am, our nephew stopped in to say hi, and we thought you'd like to meet him," Marjorie said as Elise came into the kitchen.

She spotted Zach sitting there first, and a puzzled look crossed her face. Then she turned to greet their nephew. Instantly she froze in her tracks, frowned deeply and stared at him for what seemed to be an incredibly long time. "Oh my God I know you! Bastian! Bastian!" She ran to him as he jumped up to give her a bone breaking hug.

"Elise! It is you, oh my girl! You're alive! I went to your funeral!" He hugged her tight and didn't want to let her go. Neither did she. She buried her face in his chest for a minute, holding him tightly. Finally they let go of each other, and Bastian looked at her closely. "I can't believe this. You look a little different, but it's you, it's my Elise."

"I knew it. I'm not crazy. I AM Elise," she said softly, turning to look at everyone in the room, "but how? Zach?"

"I told you we'd get this figured out, and finding out if you really were Elise was the first step. You obviously are, which is a great relief," Zach smiled. "I told Marjorie and Marie about your predicament earlier and they were more than happy to help out. They already had their doubts about you."

"I can't thank all of you enough, this is such a relief! You can't imagine how hard it is to try and remember things you never knew." Elise said as she sat down close to Bastian.

"You remembered Bastian as soon as you saw him," Zach pointed out, "so more than likely you'll remember other things that were familiar to you, once you are back in your old neighborhood, and not in a strange house."

"Yes, I'm sure I will, but my apartment, did it really burn down?" Elise asked, remembering the article in the newspapers, "and who was it that died there, if it wasn't me?"

Zach was about to answer her with what he thought was the logical answer, but was interrupted.

"Well, what a lovely little gathering, what do we have here?" A harsh voice from the doorway boomed into the room.

Chapter 7

"H…Harold, you're home early," Elise stammered. "Marjorie's and Marie's nephew and a friend of his are in town, and they surprised us with a visit. They were nice enough to introduce them both to me."

"Oh, how nice," Harold said, his tone calming down a notch or two as he turned his attention to the two men. "Where are you visiting from? Going to be in town long?"

Zach quickly replied before Bastian could. "We're from Minnesota, name's Zach, and this is Bastian, their nephew. We're only in town for a couple days."

"Haven't seen my aunts for a few years, and thought it would be nice to surprise them," Bastian added pleasantly, "hope you don't mind."

"Not at all, enjoy your visit, mind if I join you?" Harold said as he took the chair right next to Elise, her close proximity to Bastian not going unnoticed.

"Please do! Bastian was just telling his aunts that he's a professional clown, weren't you Bastian?" Zach said, continuing the charade.

"Yes I was, they were enjoying my stories about my three trained little dogs that are a part of my act," Bastian replied, smoothly going along with Zach's story.

"That is rather delightful sounding, but on second thought, I'd best get a few things taken care of in my office. Nice to meet the two of you," he said brusquely as he stood up. He planted one of his dry kisses on Elise's head and left the room. Once he was gone, they all sat in silence for a moment, exchanging nervous glances.

Finally Zach spoke. "Okay, that was awkward. Think he suspects anything?"

"I don't think so, or he wouldn't have left the room," Marjorie said, then added, "he's usually too self-absorbed to worry about what's going on in the house if it doesn't involve him."

"You may continue to enjoy your little family reunion, but I need to speak with my wife in the other room. If you'll excuse us for a moment," Harold said, returning to the room and coaxing Elise up from her chair. She gave them a raised eyebrow and followed him out of the kitchen.

Zach watched them go in silence. He ran his hand through his hair, mussing it up more than it already was. "Wonder what that's about?"

"Probably doesn't want her socializing with the hired help," Marjorie said with a deep sigh.

"Well now that we know she is Elise, I don't see any reason for her to stay here any longer," Zach said thoughtfully, "but where can she go? Her place burned to the ground."

"That's no problem, she can crash with me for a few days, and I'm sure our building manager will find her a new apartment in the complex. There's a few hundred apartments there. I hope they find her a new one close to mine again," Bastian said, more than happy to get his favorite neighbor back where she belonged.

"How will you tell Mr. R. that you want to take his wife away from here?" Marie asked, "I mean she's not his wife, but he acts like she is."

"I don't think I'd tell him anything. When she leaves, I think he'll be able to put two and two together, and figure out she did remember who she really is. She can leave a note for him. He does know she's been starting to remember things, and none of it is from here," Zach pointed out. "She can come with us now, or if she prefers, she can leave in the morning, once he goes to work, to avoid a scene with him."

"That does leave these two ladies left to clean up the mess," Bastian said softly.

"Don't worry about us! We can act stupid. We don't know nothing," Marjorie said with a big smile.

"That's right, we just clean the house, cook the meals. We don't keep track of the missus and her comings and goings," Marie added, "he might ask us if we know where she went, but we'll say no, she didn't tell us. He'll believe that, no problem."

Just then Harold returned. "My wife has gone to take a nap, she still tires easily from her ordeal. I'd like to ask you to finish your visit now, so my help here can get back to their duties." With that, he turned and left the room.

"Okay, that ends that. I'll leave you two my number so you can call me if necessary. Please tell Elise I can come and get her any time she wants, and that Bastian will be more than happy to have a house guest for a while," Zach said, standing up and handing the ladies a couple of his business cards. There wasn't much else they could do today, and he wasn't worried about Elise staying there another day or two.

Bastian wasn't in a great rush to get home. He was still incredibly hyped at seeing Elise alive! Instead he rode with Zach to Franklin, where the two of them installed a small motion sensor trail camera in a tree near Alvin Hooper's balcony. Now instead of Zach sitting there each day waiting for someone to climb onto Alvin's porch, he'd just check the camera every few days. By the time they finished that, it was time to call it a day.

Rudy was happy to see Zach after the long day, and gave him a proper German Shepherd face washing welcome. Just for good measure, he gave Bastian an equally wet welcome.

"Did Elise tell you what she does for a living? Or maybe she doesn't remember yet," Bastian said as he gave Rudy a vigorous belly rub.

"No, I don't think she remembers that yet. Hasn't mentioned anything," Zach said, furrowing his brow.

"She trains dogs. Especially difficult ones. She has clients all over the place. I bet they're all wondering what happened to her," Bastian said, "though I guess they must have read about her death in the papers."

"A dog trainer? Well, that explains her comments about living in jeans. That makes sense. I'll have to make sure she gets to meet Rudy. Maybe she can teach him some manners," Zach said, giving Rudy an affectionate pat on the side.

"Your work seems a lot more interesting than being a clown," Bastian said, looking around the efficient little office.

"It can be, but a lot of it is pretty ordinary stuff, things the police can't help much with, but people don't want to drop. Like the deal with the guy in Franklin. I'm guessing it's nothing more than a neighbor kid goofing around on Alvin's balcony. A thief would have been able to get in the first time he was there. A sliding door is about the easiest thing to open, and a home burglar would know that. Alvin would have been cheaper off spending his money on a good lock for that door, rather than hiring me, but some people don't want to hear that sort of thing. They need someone to validate their problem and help them find a solution. Sometimes they just want someone to listen to them. I guess that's why I'm always busy." Zach explained. "And of course, then there are the cases, like Elise, where she really did need some help. I enjoy those cases, where I can truly help out, make a difference, know what I mean?"

"Yeah, I do. I know you didn't dig into Elise's life for me, but I can't tell you how happy I am you found out the truth about her. I still can't believe she's alive. Man, that is awesome," Bastian shook his head in disbelief. He paused, deep in thought for a moment, "so who do you suppose the dead lady in her apartment was? Harold's wife?"

"Yeah, that's my best guess. Don't know who else it would be, and they do look very much the same. I haven't figured out how he managed the switch, or the infamous tattoo but once I get Elise out of his house, I think the rest is a police matter. They may have to exhume the body, do DNA testing on it to verify it was Melody. Hey, does Elise have any family?" the thought suddenly hit Zach.

"Oh geez! Yeah, she does. A brother and her mother, both on the east coast. They were here for the funeral. I luckily had the mother's address and phone, and called her. She called her son," Bastian replied.

"Guess you'll be making another call to her mom pretty soon," Zach smiled, "with better news this time."

"Won't that be a hell of a strange call to get!" Bastian laughed, "geez, you bury your kid then get a call a couple weeks later that it was a mistake and she's fine? When do you think I should call her, tonight?"

"Yeah, if you think she can handle it, without having Elise right there to talk to her. Tell her she'll be with you soon," Zach said, thinking it over.

"Sure thing. If I was her, I'd want to know as soon as possible. One less sleepless night thinking your daughter is dead," Bastian agreed. With that he stood to go. "I'll be taking off now. Let me know when you're getting Elise. I can drive up and take her home, anytime, man. I can even tag along when you go get her! I am available."

"Thanks Bastian, you've been a big help. I'll give you a call as soon as I know what's going on."

With that, Bastian hopped onto his Harley and was gone and Zach was left with Rudy. They went home to their apartment in Muskego. As he drove, Zach once again thought about moving closer to his office. Muskego was a nice town, but not as close as he'd like to be to his office. There weren't a lot of apartments in Brookfield that allowed large dogs, and he also needed room for when his eight year old son Nathan came to visit. Since he acquired Rudy, Nathan was anxious to come over even more than before, which was plenty. Zach smiled as he pictured Nathan and Rudy playing together. A boy and his dog. He knew Nathan's mother, Zach's ex, would never allow him to have a dog, which she called filthy animals that should be left outside. He smiled at that ridiculous thought as he gave Rudy an affection rub under his chin. At least Nathan could have a dog part of the time, whenever he was with Zach. Yes, getting a place closer to work with room for Rudy and Nathan to play needed to go to the top of his to-do list. He could have Kelly poke around and see what she could find.

At home, he fed Rudy, who was happy to retire to his roomy

crate for a nap while Zach played over the day's events. This was too easy, he thought. Tomorrow he would get Elise out of there, deliver her to Bastian, and hand the rest of it over to police. By afternoon, he'd be on another case. He kind of wished the apartment fire had been in Milwaukee, so his buddies on the police force there could be involved, and he'd be kept informed of what the heck happened there. Oh well, he sighed, another day, another case to solve, he smiled as he grabbed a beer for himself and turned on the news, and promptly dozed off.

As usual, the next morning, Rudy was waking Zach up as the sun was coming up. Apparently dogs think if there's any daylight around, everyone should be up. Reluctantly, he rubbed the sleep out of his eyes, and as he did, the phone rang.

"Marchand, what's up?" was his very unprofessional reply first thing in the morning.

"Mr. Marchand, she's gone!" came the panicked reply on the other end.

Instantly he was completely awake and standing next to his bed. "Gone? Who, Elise?" he barked into the phone.

"Yes, Mr. Marchand, she is gone. I check on her this morning, and her bed is empty. Some of her things are gone too, some clothing, toiletries, all gone." Marie burst out, almost out of breath, "the mister is gone too, but I don't know if they went together, maybe he went to work."

"Go have another look around her room, and in her study, see if there are any clues," Zach instructed her, his mind racing.

"Okay, I'll go look at everything," she said, apparently setting the phone down to do so. Shortly she returned, "I don't see anything like a clue. Some of her clothes are gone, her toiletries, but her laptop is still on her desk. I don't see anything else wrong. Now what do we do Mr. Marchand?"

"Don't do anything yet, let me check a few things. I'll get back to you. Don't do anything, don't call anyone," he repeated as he hung up the phone.

What the hell was going on now? Did she decide to leave last night, maybe called a cab? Zach wracked his brain for anything that might make sense, but came up blank. Surely if she remembered where her apartment was, she'd go there and Bastian would have called him. He called Bastian, waking him out of a sound sleep.

"What the heck time is it?" came a sleepy voice.

"Bastian, it's Zach. Elise is gone. Did she come by you last night or this morning?" Zach asked, afraid he already knew the answer.

"Here, no, I crashed when I got back from your place, the phone ringing is the first thing I've encountered since then. You're telling me she left that place, without letting you know where she was going? That doesn't make sense," Bastian said, waking up completely.

"It looks like that might be the case. But if she didn't call me or you, or come to your place, where else would she have gone? And why didn't she let either of us know what's going on?" Zach questioned, "unless she didn't go willingly...."

"I'm on my way!" Bastian said as he jumped out of bed and scrambled to get some clothes on. "Figure something out and I'll be there in twenty minutes!"

Unfortunately, Zach didn't know what he was going to figure out in twenty minutes. Would it do any good to go talk to the sisters at Harold's place? What else was there to do? He was still mulling this over in his head as he drove to his office. He parked and was about to unlock the door when he realized it was already unlocked.

Entering his business, he was surprised to see Kelly already there. "Do you ever go home?"

"I like to come in early and make sure things are in order for the day," Kelly said with a smile as she handed him a cup of very welcome coffee. He barely had time to take it from her, when the door burst open.

"Bastian has arrived!" he said as he burst through the door, "what's the game plan?"

"Sadly, there isn't one yet. Other than talking to the sisters again, which may be pointless, what can we do?" Zach shook his head sadly. "I'm pretty sure asking Harold where she is isn't going to work. Can't report her missing to the police."

"Why not call old Harold, and ask if we can have lunch with her before we leave town?" Bastian suggested.

"Not a bad idea, but he'd probably say no, since you're just the hired help's nephew. Maybe Kelly should call and say she's an old friend in town and wants to have lunch with her," Zach said, turning to look at Kelly.

Kelly shrugged, dug out the number for Harold's law office and dialed. After getting transferred only twice, she was surprised to actually get Harold himself on the other end.

"Hi, Harold, I don't know if Melody ever mentioned me, my name's Kelly. We took a few horticultural classes together a number of years ago, and we really hit it off. I promised her if I was ever in the area, I'd give her a call." Kelly invented her story as she spoke, "I'm in town for only a couple days, from New York, and wondered if she'd be available for lunch? I can't find her home phone number, but I did remember her telling me her husband was a pretty successful attorney. Can you get me in touch with her?"

"I don't really recall Melody mentioning you, but she does

enjoy classes like that. However, your timing is a bit unfortunate, I'm afraid," Harold spoke crisply. "Melody was in an automobile accident a few weeks ago, with numerous injuries, as well as some short term amnesia. I doubt she'd even remember you at this point in her recovery."

"Oh, I'm so sorry to hear that. Is she in the hospital? Maybe I could pop in for just a quick visit?" Kelly persisted.

"Sorry, not possible. Unfortunately, Melody took a turn for the worse just last night and has been re-hospitalized. She is not receiving any visitors at this time. Now if you'll excuse me," Harold finished.

"Can you give me a phone number, so I can give her a call sometime?" Kelly made one last effort to get any information she could.

"I'm sorry, I don't give out her number to anyone who calls. I'll tell her you called and she can contact you if she likes. Good day." There was a loud click and the phone went dead.

"Well, that didn't do much good," Kelly said dejectedly as she set the phone back on its cradle.

"Not much, but he did say she took a turn for the worse and was taken back to the hospital," Zach said, "I wonder if that was true? Do we have the name of that private hospital she was taken to after the accident?"

"No, we don't. It wasn't in the police report or in the news. But how many private hospitals can there be in Oconomowoc?" Kelly started searching online as she spoke. "Hmmm, I don't see any small private hospitals listed here for Oconomowoc, or anywhere close to it. How small is this place it's not even listed online as a hospital?"

"Wonder if it's more of a clinic, with a few beds? Very small?"

Zach suggested. "Maybe affiliated with one of the doctors caring for her? I'll give Marie a call and see if there are any prescription bottles or other clues at the house. Maybe we can find the name of any doctors who treated her."

Before he could make the call, the cell phone in his pocket sounded. He grabbed it and turned it on. It was Elise texting him!

"H took me from house last night - location unknown, 20 min ride. more when I know anything. don't reply."

"I knew it! That jerk took her! At least we know she's okay, more or less," Zach said, feeling the blood rushing through his veins. He'd have to wait for word from her, which was going to be difficult.

"It's something, but what now?" Bastian asked, pacing and anxious to do something.

"Here's a map of his house and a circle around it, all the places you could drive to in 20-25 minutes. Let's see if there are any clinics or health care facilities around," Kelly said as she pulled up a map online and made a big red circle around it.

"Time for a ride!" Zach motioned for Bastian to follow him, knowing Kelly would keep digging and if she found anything she'd let him know.

For the next hour or more, they drove around Delafield, Oconomowoc, Pewaukee, and surrounding areas, searching for small clinics, urgent care facilities or anything that might have a few hospital beds. Kelly kept feeding them possible locations, but they were all dead ends.

"What if a doctor has something set up right in his home? Like you see in old movies?" Bastian suggested, knowing it was a real leap.

"Gee, that would be great, then all we need to do is check out every doctor within 20 miles of Harold's house," Zach groaned. "Let's hope that isn't the case."

He called Marie and asked if there were any prescription bottles still in the bedroom. She looked around and told him there was nothing. Whatever she had must have been packed up and taken with her. Another dead end, Zach mumbled to himself and rubbed his neck where the muscles were tightening. Just then his phone rang.

"Mr. Marchand, I find one empty bottle from pills in trash. For Melody, and from Doctor Mathias." Marie said as she spelled the doctor's name for him.

"Marie, that's great! Good thinking to check the trash. Hang tight, we'll get this all figured out," Zach told her. By the time he hung up, Kelly was already searching for the doctor online.

"Raymond Mathias is a retired general practitioner, no mention of where he ever practiced though," Kelly read as she searched, "let me see if I can find out where he lives or anything."

"That would be too easy," Zach laughed, "what, did you say he's a GP? I would have thought she'd be under the care of a neurologist with brain injury, or a plastic surgeon, not a general practitioner. Something isn't quite adding up."

"Hmm, that is odd, isn't it? Let me see what else I can find. Here we go, he worked at St. Luke's in Milwaukee for a number of years, until he lost his license several years ago. Not a lot of info on that…… enjoying his imposed retirement at his home on Lake Nagawicka. No address, though." Kelly said, looking away from her monitor. "I'll do a little more digging and see what I can come up with."

"Good idea, and I'll go check my camera in Franklin," Zach sighed slowly. "Bastian, feel like climbing a tree again?"

The hidden camera turned out to be a good idea. Zach inserted the SD card into his laptop to have a look at what they might have caught on camera. The SD card had a number of photos on it. Since it was a motion sensor camera, there were a lot of blowing leaves and a few squirrels and birds that got close to the lens. But the porch climbing culprit was plainly visible too. Alvin was not going to be too impressed. It was a large tom cat. It hopped onto the porch railing, hopped onto the table on the balcony, then onto the balcony floor. He knocked over a few pots, and the noise apparently scared him off. End of mystery. If only they were all so easy.

"I'll let Alvin know what we got here. Pretty disappointing for a guy looking for seriously interesting criminal activity," Zach said as Bastian helped him remove the camera from the tree. This little gadget could come in handy again. As they were debating about somewhere to grab a bite to eat, he got another message from Elise.

"*In a basement, a house, windows boarded, not taking my pills. someone is here most of the time. Dr from accident here. More when I can.*"

Chapter 8

Elise lay motionless in the hospital style bed. She could hear machinery running near her, but was pretty sure nothing was attached to her. It all seemed to be connected to the still figure in the bed several feet from her. Elise only dared a few quick peeks when she was certain she was alone, but she was pretty sure the other person was Harold's real wife. What had they done to Melody? And what were they planning to do to her? How was she going to get out of here? She was so rarely alone. Right now, there were two men in the room, on the other side of the screened panels next to her bed. Their conversation was whispered, but animated. She strained to make out what they were saying. She was pretty sure one of them was Harold.

"I have to be careful to give her just the right amount so she can still function but not remember anything. Too much of her memory has returned already, so I've increased it a little," the first man said.

"Why can't you just up the dose more? How hard is that?" The man Elise thought was Harold said in a very irate tone.

"We both know what happened when I upped the dose too

quickly the last time," the first man said again, "I think I have to increase the dose a lot slower, and the pill form seems to work better for her."

"How much longer before you get her out of her stupor so we can start working on her new memories? We don't have forever you know, people are starting to wonder where my wife is. I can't offer lame excuses forever," Harold said.

"Soon, very soon. She wakes up easily to take her pills and offers no resistance. She hasn't asked where she is or why she's here, so we're making good progress. Very soon her mind will be a blank slate for me to imprint whatever we like on it," the first man calmly spoke.

"All right, that sounds good. And don't forget, I want her anxious to get pregnant and start a family. Make sure that's drilled into her brain," Harold stated without emotion.

"I understand….like I said, soon her mind will be a blank slate and we can put whatever we want in it," the man said, speaking softly and hesitantly, as if he was doing something he didn't want to be doing.

"Just get it taken care of, and soon. I'm not paying you a fortune to make another brain dead zombie."

It was all Elise could do to lie still and not make a sound as she heard their plans for her. She needed to get out of here, and soon. Anxious to start a family? And with no memory? She felt the small pile of pills she had stuck into the corner of her pillowcase. Thank God she thought to spit them out from the beginning. The two men were still talking, but now moved closer to her bed, within a few feet. Elise kept her eyes closed and breathed slowly. She had no idea how she was supposed to act on the drugs she'd been given, but she was hoping sleepy and docile were convincing. She heard them doing something to the bed next to her. Machines were adjusted and their sounds changed slightly.

"What about her? We can't leave her like this forever," Harold said, with as much emotion as if he was speaking about a bag of trash.

"We won't have to worry, her brain waves are dying gradually. A few more days she'll be flatlined," the doctor said, "then you'll merely have a body to dispose of."

Elise swallowed hard, and clenched her fists under the sheets, feeling the cell phone she had slid into the back of her panties. She needed to get out of here, and wasn't going to be able to wait for Zach to find and rescue her.

*　　*　　*　　*　　*

"Now we're getting somewhere, she's in a house," Zach said as he read the message, "and most likely, the doctor she mentioned is Raymond Mathias. That still bugs me. General practitioners don't treat someone after a brain injury. What the hell am I missing here?"

"That does sound strange. With a bad concussion, a neurologist would be looking at her," Bastian agreed, playing with his long braid absentmindedly. "What are we going to do now? I hate knowing she's out there alone and we can't do a thing to help her!"

"Yeah, there's always something we can do to help, we just haven't figured out what it is yet," Zach said thoughtfully. "I think I need Kelly to check something out for me. Just a hunch."

They grabbed a quick bite to eat at one of those family restaurants where the food was pretty mediocre but edible, and always served in vast quantities. Zach had his leftovers bagged up for Rudy, and as they were leaving, Kelly called.

"You were right, the good Doctor Mathias has gotten several speeding tickets in one of his three fancy-schmancy cars. It's on Lake Nagawicka, in Hartland. I looked it up online, it's at the end of a dead end street, looks like a pretty wooded area," Kelly said, giving him the address.

"You're a doll, Kelly, what would I do without you?" Zach scribbled the address on the back of his receipt.

"Ha! You'll never know," her smile was evident through the phone.

"Looks like a ride to Hartland is next on the agenda!" Zach said, excited to have something concrete to work on. Rudy happily chomped down the remnants of a steak sandwich and settled down on the back seat for a nap.

"Got any plans for what we do when we get to the doc's house? Can't just charge in like the calvary and rescue her," Bastian asked.

"I've got a few tricks up my sleeve for that. There's an ID tag and a clipboard from a pest control company in the glovebox. Most people won't let you in their house, but they'll usually allow you to walk around the outside. I can look for boarded up windows, to make sure we've got the right place," Zach explained. "Then I'll come back later, when it's dark out, and see if I can get in there."

"You mean we, don't you?" Bastian corrected him. "You don't think I'm going to just drive home and sit there and wait for Elise to appear do you? Really man?"

"I usually work alone," Zach said thoughtfully, "don't want to put anyone else at risk. I can't protect you in a situation like this."

"Hell Zach, you have no idea what you'll encounter if you manage to get into that basement. I may look a little unconventional, but you want me on your side. I have a third-degree black belt in karate, I might come in handy in that basement," Bastian said without bravado.

Zach let out a low whistle. "In that case, you can come along and protect me."

They found the address Kelly had given them, and she was spot on with her assessment of the area, thanks to the satellite maps she had been looking at. Zach flashed his pest control badge at the housekeeper who answered the door. That along with a charming smile, and he was told to go ahead and check the exterior for suspected termites.

He made a slow circle of the house, shining a flashlight along the foundation, and trying to look thorough in case anyone was watching him. The casement windows were larger than normal, with window wells dug deeper into the ground than usual, allowing a lot more light into the basement. That is, if they weren't all boarded up. Every window in the basement had been boarded up. Why bother making larger windows if you're going to board them up? As with everything else in this case, things didn't add up. He returned to his truck and informed Bastian of his findings.

They waited until it was completely dark out before returning to the Mathias home. Zach parked a few houses away and they crept unseen through the trees, to the dark side of the house closest to the wooded area. No other homes were visible from here. He aimed the low beam of a flashlight at one of the wood covered windows, to show Bastian how they had been boarded up.

"This wasn't a rush job either, the wood was all cut to fit the frames perfectly, and even painted to match the rest of the trim," he pointed out.

Bastian knelt down for a closer look. "This is interesting, shine that thing down here, look at this. Screws. The boards are screwed right onto the window frame, from the outside."

"Jesus, that means they weren't here to keep anything or anyone out, but to keep them in. Shit. Looks like we got the right house," Zach hissed. "Alright, here's the plan. You go to the front door, distract anyone who's home for a few minutes, while I get one of these windows uncovered. Can you do that?"

"Hell yes, got a perfect plan. Be careful." Bastian said with a big smile.

Zach pulled a screwdriver out of the small sack he brought with him, and started on the first long screw. He watched Bastian walk out to the road and then turn down the Mathias driveway. He wondered what sort of plan he had come up with so quickly.

Bastian rang the doorbell and put an anxious look on his face. Before long, the housekeeper answered the door. "How can I help you? We aren't buying anything."

"No, please, my little dog ran off, and I was hoping someone around here had seen her," Bastian said. He made a production out of pulling out his smart phone and showing her numerous pictures of his little dogs. "It's this one, Trixie, she was wearing a striped purple sweater. I stopped to get gas and she jumped out the door. She's never done that before, the naughty little girl. I saw her go running in this direction, so I'm asking everyone around here if they've seen her."

"Oh my, such a tiny dog!" the housekeeper said, looking at all the pictures. "No, I haven't seen that little thing at all. Poor baby, she will get so cold out here tonight."

"Yes I know, I am frantic to find her," Bastian continued, "is there anyone else home that might have seen her? Anyone?"

"Doctor is home, but he is busy in the basement. But I don't think he would see a little doggy," she said hesitantly.

"Could you go ask him, please? Just in case he saw her running across the yard or anything? It might point me in the right direction."

"Okay, I guess I can do that. You please wait here," she said as she closed the front door in his face. She came back only a few minutes later. "He said no, he didn't see any little dog, but you better hope she isn't dinner for one of the coyotes out here."

"Okay, thank you so much for your time, I'll keep asking around," Bastian nodded and left. He made a show of walking down to the road and up the next driveway, then crept through the dark yards to where Zach had been working on the window. Zach was just pulling out the final screw when Bastian stooped next to him, and pulled his arm away from the board.

"How'd it go?" Zach asked quietly.

"Sounded like only the housekeeper and the doc are in the house, but she said he was in the basement," Bastian said with a frustrated frown.

"Damn, not a good time for us to make our move. How are we going to get him out of there?" Zach said, taking his hands off the wooden panel. He ran his fingers through his hair, trying to think. "I wonder if Marie could call him from Harold's house and say Harold wants him to come over? I hate to get her in trouble with him, but maybe she could pull it off."

They made their way back to the truck, where Zach called Marie and asked her if she could do what he asked. He made a point of telling her he didn't want to get her in any trouble. She just laughed heartily.

"Mister thinks we are all stupid Mexicans, he'll think I just messed up a phone message. I will act like the fool he thinks I am. It is fun to trick him, he thinks he is so smart. And I want to help the missus." She chuckled the whole time she spoke. "I will call the doctor right now, his number is in the phone. And then I will answer all calls, in case he calls back to check with the mister."

Zach thanked her profusely, and they drove away. He didn't want the doctor noticing his truck on the road, even if it wasn't right in front of his house. He drove down the block and around the corner. He could still see the Mathias house. They sat there in the dark truck, waiting for something to happen. Suddenly there was a tap on the window.

"Can I ask why you are parked here?" an elderly man with a cane and a shaggy dog on a leash inquired of them.

"Oh sorry, didn't mean to bother anyone," Zach started to say, not sure what to tell the guy.

"Looking for my lost little dog," Bastian finished for him. He quickly pulled out his phone and showed several pictures to the man. "We were just crossing off the houses where we already asked about her."

"It's awfully dark out here to be looking for a dog," he said dubiously.

Zach turned his attention to the intersection ahead. He couldn't help but notice the sleek white jaguar as it barely slowed at the stop sign. It turned and disappeared down the road. He turned to see the garage door closing on the Mathias house. They needed to get over there, fast.

"It is dark out, we know, but we've been looking for her all day." Bastian used the most forlorn tone of voice he could manage. "Can't imagine leaving her out here alone all night, we'll search all night if we have to. We'll find her. You didn't happen to see her, did you? She's wearing a purple striped sweater."

"Well, no, can't say that I did. Buster here would have raised a ruckus if another dog had been nearby," he told Bastian. "Well, good luck to you, don't know how you'll find a small dog like that in the middle of the night though." The old man shook his head as he walked away.

"Thanks, that was close. My mind sort of went blank," Zach admitted, "I was watching the doc's garage door. He just left. We need to be quick about this, let's go." Once again he parked down the road from the Mathias home, and they crept silently through the trees to the back of the house.

Immediately they both noticed light coming from one of the basement windows. They looked at each other, puzzlement obvious on their faces. "That's the board I had loose," Zach said quietly, "was just taking the last screws out when you stopped me. The board must have just fallen off."

"Yeah, it's lying right here," Bastian agreed, trying to peer into the basement.

"There's obviously a light on down there," Zach said, sticking his head into the window well. He could see a well lit room with some office style chairs, a desk and bright floor lamps. There didn't appear to be anyone around. "Well, here goes nothing," he said as he eased himself into the window well.

"Watch yourself," Bastian cautioned from right behind him.

Zach crouched low in the window well and stuck his head into the basement. To the right were the chairs and desk he had already seen, and to the left were hospital style privacy screens on wheels. There were several of them blocking off his view of the rest of the basement, but they were somewhat translucent. Translucent enough to make out several large objects that could be beds. He hopped out of the window and down into the room, which was only about a four foot jump. Almost silently, Bastian was right behind him. Zach motioned for him to stay where he was as he moved quietly to the first screen. He pulled it back, revealing 4 hospital beds in a row. Next to each bed stood a small nightstand, some holding monitoring equipment of some sort, with various wires and dials connected to them. Above each bed there was a monitor attached to the wall. All but one of the monitors was blank. There were several other pieces of equipment, on wheeled carts near the beds. Three of the beds were empty. In the bed furthest from them, with the live monitor, they could see a still figure lying there. Bastian moved closer and let out a quiet little gasp.

"Oh my God, I thought that was Elise! But it's not, is it?" He leaned a bit closer and looked at the woman lying there.

"No, it's not Elise, she still has a bit of her injuries visible, remember? This has to be the real Melody! Holy shit, what have they done to her? She looks like she's in a coma," Zach said in a shocked whisper. "And where the hell is Elise? She must have been here."

He pointed to the first bed they had stepped past, where the rumpled bedding looked like someone had just gotten out of it.

"Shit, she was here! Did he take her with him?" Zach hissed, "damn! We were that close!"

"Oh crap, yeah, she was here," Bastian muttered, feeling the still warm sheets. As he did, his hand bumped something. It was a cell phone, "this look familiar?"

Chapter 9

"Awww, crap, yeah, that's the phone I gave her." Zach groaned as he paced around the room. "Shit! Shit! We were only minutes from her! Where's he taking her now? Back to Harold?"

"And now she has no way to contact us," Bastian said dejectedly.

"Wait! Look at this," Zach said, pointing to the window they had just climbed through. There was a small torn piece of fabric hanging from a sharp corner of the window frame. "She must have climbed out here. She probably heard me unscrewing the board."

"If that's the case, she didn't leave that long ago. We might be able to find her!" Bastian burst out, heading for the window.

They both quickly climbed back out the way they had gotten in, and Zach put the board back against the opening. He hurriedly turned a few of the screws in by hand, just enough to hold the board in place, and look like the whole thing was undisturbed. They ran back to the truck, calling Elise's name as they ran. She was nowhere to be seen. They drove around for close to an hour, without luck. Elise was not to be found.

*   *   *   *   *   *

Elise laid quietly in the sterile, hospital-like basement room. The woman in the other bed didn't move or respond, but Elise could still hear the rhythmic hiss of the ventilator she was hooked up to. The doctor had been down here a few minutes ago, but he seemed to have left suddenly, and she was pretty sure she heard the garage door open and close. She wasn't positive, but she thought she also heard someone at one of the basement windows. She had been given pills regularly, the same ones that had kept her mind so foggy ever since we woke up in Harold's house. Except now, she only pretended to take them, then hid them inside her pillowcase. She always made sure to act drugged and lethargic or sleeping when anyone was in the room. But now, she was pretty sure she was alone, save for the other woman. Silently she slid out of the bed, walking as carefully as she could with the clunky cast on her foot, and peered through the narrow gab between two of the privacy screens. No one was there, but she definitely could hear something happening by one of the windows. She stood motionless in the corner, waiting to see if anything was going to happen. She hoped it was Zach on the other side, but had no idea.

After a few minutes, the sounds stopped. She waited a few minutes longer, and still nothing happened. Quietly, she stepped to the boarded up window. The large casement window was less than four feet from the ground, and she could easily reach the latch to open it. Beyond the open window was the large board. Had someone loosened it? Or had they been reinforcing it? She gave it a slight shove and it fell out! She gave a quick startled gasp, took a last look behind her and managed to crawl out. She was free!

It was totally dark out, and this side of the house faced several unimproved lots, still densely tree covered. She hurried into the cover of the trees and had a look around. She realized she forgot the cell phone Zach had given her, but there was no way she was going back for it. She needed to get to a phone and call him. No way was she going to knock on the door of one of the doctor's neighbors. She needed to find a gas station or convenience store, or anything that might be open. It was cold out, but she wasn't concerned with the weather. She'd find a phone, call Zach and would be inside somewhere safe soon enough. She walked through the wooded area until she got to the first street. It looked completely residential in either direction, and in reality, she had no idea what city she was even in. She decided to go to the right, mainly because it seemed to be taking her farther from the doctor's house. She walked along the shoulder of the road for a couple blocks. It was slow going with the cumbersome cast on her right foot and only a rubber soled sock on her left. Not a lot of protection from the rocks and stones along the shoulder. Suddenly, she saw the headlights of a car coming up behind her. She stopped, wondering how stupid it would be to hitch a ride.

"Ma'am, are you all right?" The police patrol car drove up close to her and the officer inside rolled his window down.

"Yes, I'm fine, just trying to get to a phone. I forgot mine," she said, knowing it sounded pretty lame.

"It's pretty late and cold to be out walking around dressed like that," the officer said, keeping pace with her walking. "Maybe you'd like a ride somewhere?"

"No, but do you have a phone I could use?"

"I can get you to a phone, but can you tell me where you're trying to go? Did you just leave a hospital?" The officer asked in a pleasant voice, but it was obvious he wasn't going away unless he got some satisfactory answers.

"It's kind of a long complicated story. I was being held in a house against my will, and I just managed to get out. I need to call Zach and have him come and get me," Elise burst out, not wanting to go into the whole story.

"Held against your will? Were you kidnapped? What's your name?" The officer was pretty sure she was confused or maybe high on something.

"Umm, my name is Elise. Elise Taggert. Yes, I was sort of kidnapped, I guess, I'm not sure," she was getting so frustrated trying to make sense and making it all sound worse and worse.

"Okay, maybe we should take a ride to the station and get you something warm to wear, maybe something to eat, and you can give your friend a call," the officer said as he stopped the car. He plugged in her name and the first thing that came up was her obituary and the article about the apartment fire. He got out and helped her into the back seat.

Elise gave a long sigh. This wasn't what she had planned on, but at least she could call Zach once they got to the police station. As she sat in the back, she couldn't help but hear the officer talking to dispatch about picking up a caucasian female, confused, possible psych eval. She sighed again. "I'm not crazy, I've had a bad day, that's all, and I need to make a phone call."

"That's all right ma'am, we'll be at the station in just a few, hang tight," the officer said as he drove, "we can get everything straightened out there."

Elise sighed again and stared out the window. She figured anything she said would only make her sound more like a crazy lady. Everything was coming out all wrong. She leaned back in the seat and slumped down.

At the Delafield police station, the officer who picked her up took her into an interview room, placed a bottle of water on the table and put a blanket around her shoulders. "I'm going to get someone in here to talk to you. We'll get everything straightened out, and you can make your phone call."

She sat quietly, hoping this wouldn't take very long. All she wanted to do was call Zach and get her out of here. Moments later, a female officer came into the room.

"Hi, I'm Officer Patricia Lang, are you comfortable? Warm enough? Are you hungry?" She asked in a very kind and comforting tone.

"I'm good, thanks. I don't really need to be here, I just need to make a phone call. Can I do that?" Elise asked.

"Yes of course, let me ask you a few quick questions first. This won't take long," Officer Lang said with a smile. "First of all, can you tell me your name?"

"Of course. It's Elise Taggert."

"And where do you live, Elise?"

"In Waukesha, at 1034 Buckley St, well, I did until recently. Then there was a fire, now I'll need a new apartment," Elise said, knowing how totally stupid it sounded. "Look, can I just call Zach? He can explain all of this."

"Okay, Elise here is the problem we have. There was a fire at that address a few weeks ago, and someone died in that fire. Her name was Elise Taggert. Do you see why we're a little concerned here? You're wearing a hospital gown, and your foot is in a cast. Where were you coming from when Officer Thompson picked you up? Were you in a hospital?" Officer Lang still spoke in a kind voice but it was obvious she was getting a little impatient.

"Look, I know everything I say is making me sound like a

nutcase, but it's a long complicated story. I am Elise Taggert, and I don't know who the woman was that died in my apartment. I was in an accident and broke my foot. I was at the home of the doctor who was looking after me after the accident. He has sort of a place in his basement for a few patients. When he left tonight, I escaped by climbing out a window. Yes it all sounds stupid, but I can't help that, it's the truth," Elise blurted out, getting it all out as quickly as she could.

"Alright, we can look into some of those details for you. What was the doctor's name who was caring for you, do you remember that?" Officer Lang asked, leaning a little closer.

"Yes, it was Dr. Mathias, Raymond Mathias. He's the one who was looking after my concussion." Elise spoke clearly, trying make the police woman see she was not crazy or confused or unstable.

"If he was caring for you, why did you climb out the window? You aren't making any sense here, Elise," the officer said with a small sigh.

"Okay, I haven't done anything wrong. I didn't break any laws. I don't have to stay here, you can't hold me can you?" Elise asked, standing up from the chair.

"Well, actually we can if we think you might need to be under the care or supervision of someone or be a danger to yourself or others," Officer Lang said, gently coaxing Elise back into her chair. "Let's just talk a little more and see if we can get this all straightened out. Can you tell me who this Zach is you want to call? Is he your husband? Boyfriend?"

"Oh no, Zach Marchand is a private investigator that I hired. That doesn't sound good I know, but he is," Elise said, shaking her head. "I called him to help me get my life straightened out. Someone has messed it up and I want my life back."

"So you need to call the private investigator you hired to help you get your life back. Who took it from you? Did you lose it in the fire?" the officer prodded, trying to get a clearer picture of what she was dealing with.

"No. You don't understand. It's very complicated. It's a huge mess. Zach can explain it." Elise crossed her arms and sat back in the chair. "I'm not talking any more until I can call Zach."

"I have only a few more questions," the officer said.

"Not saying anything else," Elise shook her head. Officer Lang sat there for a moment, then got up and left the room. Elise sat unmoving, knowing someone was watching her from the other side of the one-way glass. She wondered how she should behave, to appear as normal as possible. She decided to do absolutely nothing. If that wasn't normal, too bad.

Officer Lang returned, her brow furrowed. "I looked up a few things, Elise, if that's what you want to be called. The woman who died in that apartment fire was identified without question. How do you suppose that would be possible if you're sitting right here?"

"She was identified by the tattoo on her right calf. She was identified by my best friend who lives just down the hall. His name is Bastian Anders. Call him and ask him. He'll tell you he made a mistake, I've talked to him since the fire. In fact, he's helping Zach help me!" Elise said, her voice getting higher with each word.

"Did you know the doctor treating you isn't a practicing doctor anymore? His license was revoked several years ago. Why would you be under the care of an unlicensed doctor?"

"I don't know, I didn't know that about him. Harold must know him, I guess. He's the one who told me Dr. Mathias was treating my concussion," Elise said, puzzled.

"Who is Harold? Should we call him? Is he your husband?"

Officer Lang asked.

"No! Don't call him, he's the one who took me in the first place. He pretends I'm his wife, but I'm not. I'm not married. He calls me Melody, but I'm not Melody....do you see what I mean about this being too complicated?" Elise said with a frustrated wave of her hands.

"It certainly is. And frankly, the more information you give me, the less sense it makes. I'm going to have to call either your husband or your doctor to come and get you, unless there's someone else I can release you to. A close relative perhaps?" Officer Lang said, trying to be kind. This woman's rantings had a vaguely familiar sound to it. Could this be the same woman who had called the department a week or so ago, she wondered?

"Release me to Zach, he will vouch for me, please!!" Elise begged, "just let me call him, you can talk to him. You call him! He will make you understand all of this. I am not crazy. Please."

"All right, I'm going to call your private investigator, and have a talk with him. He's probably not at his office at this time of night though, it may have to wait until morning."

"No, call him on his cell phone, I have the number in my phone...oh, no, I forgot to bring it with me, or I would have called him long ago." With a sinking feeling, Elise realized that even if she had found a phone, she couldn't call Zach.

Chapter 10

"Wait! I have it, try calling Bastian, he might be with Zach, and if not, he'll know Zach's cell number. I do remember Bastian's number, he's been a good friend for several years."

"All right, I'll try this, but I want you to know if I can't reach someone who will take responsibility for you, and you don't want your doctor or Harold called, I will have no choice but to have you taken to Country Memorial for a psychiatric evaluation. Do you understand that?" Officer Lang said as she rose from the table. She took the number Elise gave her and left the room.

It seemed to Elise it was taking forever for anyone to come back and talk to her. How could they hold her like this? She wasn't crazy. Could they stop her if she just walked out of the room and out the building? She hadn't broken any laws. Finally the door opened and Officer Lang walked in, followed closely by Zach and Bastian!

"Oh my God am I happy to see the two of you!" Elise said with a huge sigh of relief. She hugged Bastian tightly and even gave Zach a hug. "They're practically trying to get me committed! How did you get here so fast?"

"We've been driving around the neighborhood for the last few hours, looking for you. We saw the board in the window was knocked out and figured you must have crawled out," Bastian said.

He was interrupted by Officer Lang. "Wait a minute, you mean everything she's been telling me really happened? It's true? Anyone want to fill me in on the details?"

"I can, but you'll have a hard time believing it," Zach said, and he proceeded to explain the whole scenario to her from the time he got the first phone call until they got to the station.

"Well, that's a hell of a tale. If even half of it's true it's an incredible story. But it leaves a lot of questions unanswered. Like where is this Harold's real wife? How did he manage to grab Elise here at her accident? How did he manage to find someone who conveniently looked like his wife? Who died in her apartment fire? Any ideas?" She asked as she turned off the recorder and sat back in her chair.

"Lots of ideas, nothing solid though. I have a buddy in homicide that's looking into who the woman in the fire might have been. As for where Harold's wife is, I'm guessing she's the other woman that we saw in Dr. Mathias' basement. She looked pretty rough, hooked up to a lot of equipment. Why or how he grabbed Elise, we have no idea yet," Zach told her, "now can we get her out of here?"

"Yes, of course, she's free to go." Officer Lang turned to Elise, "I'm sorry for all of this, I hope you get things straightened out."

They quickly left the building and got into Zach's truck. "I need two quick stops," Elise said as she climbed in, "a 24 hour store for some clothes and shoes, and an urgent care clinic to get this cast taken off." Once that was taken care of, Elise's hunch seemed to be right about her leg. It was apparent that her foot was not broken. The cast was there to hide her tattoo. While they waited in the clinic, she filled them in on everything she heard the two men talking about, including Melody's soon demise and the fact that Harold wanted Elise to want to start a family right away.

"Holy shit, what else is going on? How is any of this making sense?" Zach shook his head. "One of us is going to have to stay close to you for a while, until we figure out what his game is. I don't trust him at all. What's he going to do when he finds out you escaped?"

They decided it was a good time to take Elise and Bastian back to Bastian's apartment in Waukesha. They could get some sleep and tomorrow Bastian would go with her to the manager's office and see about a new apartment for her. Bastian promised not to let her out of his sight. Meanwhile, Zach had some serious investigating to do as soon as he got a few hours of sleep.

They spent the next few days helping to get Elise settled again. First, she made calls to her family, who were more than delighted to hear from her. Amid lots of tears and laughs, they made plans for a visit in the very near future.

The long term effects of the drugs she had been taking had not worn off completely, so Elise's memory was still a little hazy in some areas. It was getting better every day, and seeing familiar things in her life helped. The apartment building manager was shocked but happy to see her alive. He was only days way from finishing the renovations on her burnt out apartment, so she was thrilled to hear she could have the same unit back - only all brand new. Then, after proving to her insurance company that she was alive, she was able to get a check for all her belongings. It didn't take her long to get some new furnishings ordered. Her little Neon car was still in the parking lot behind the building. Her brother had been intending to come and sell it, but luckily for Elise, he hadn't had time to do it yet. All it needed was new keys made.

The hardest things to replace were her laptop and smart phone. All her client files were in them, so she didn't even have phone numbers or addresses for any of them. All she could do was drive around to each of them as she remembered them, and stop in and tell them in person that she was still alive and very much looking forward to working with them again. They were of course, all shocked, but thrilled to see her, and happy to resume their dog training lessons.

All the time Elise was doing this, with Bastian's help and constant company, Zach was busy trying to figure out how Elise happened to be in that accident, when she wasn't even in her own car. And how did Harold know about it so fast, getting her transferred out of Summit Medical Center almost as soon as she got there? He wondered what doctor signed off on her that fast. He decided to take a run over to the medical center and see if he could get any information there. Lucky for him it was a slow day in the ER, and right away he found one of the nurses that had some time to talk to him.

"This happened a few weeks ago, but is there possibly anyone here that remembers an accident where a woman was brought in and almost immediately transferred to another hospital. Does that happen a lot?"

"No it doesn't really, unless there's a good reason for the move," one very young looking nurse told him. She looked like she could be a high school cheerleader, with a blonde ponytail and bright blue eyes. "In fact, until a patient has been assessed, it's rather dangerous to move them, especially after an accident. There is the risk of neck and spinal injuries. But to your question, I have no knowledge of that accident. Probably off that day. Do you happen to know exactly what day it was?"

"Yes, it was a Friday evening, May first." Zach said.

"Let me check something," she said as she quickly flicked through a hanging file. "Looks like Lydia worked that night, she's over there, in the zebra print top, she might remember something about that accident." Cheerleader pointed to a large dark skinned woman seated at a small desk on the other side of the room. He thanked her for the help and went to see Lydia.

Lydia was furiously charting as he approached, and immediately held up her hand to stop him before he got started. After a few minutes, she finally looked up. "Sorry, got to write it down while it's fresh in my mind. How can I help you?"

"I'm trying to find anyone who was here the night a friend of mine was brought in from an auto accident. It was May first, in the evening. Almost as soon as she got here, her husband had her transferred out. Do you remember anything about that?" Zach asked hopefully.

"Honey, do I ever! That was the strangest thing. Young woman came in on the stretcher, completely out of it. Had some bruising on her face, bloody nose, but no visible gross injuries. Our resident on call, Dr. Woods, didn't even have a chance to evaluate her, and this crazy guy and his doctor buddy come running in right behind the EMTs who brought her in. Said they need her transferred to a private hospital where they can watch her more closely. Guy was a real jerk, you know what I'm saying?" Lydia became quite agitated as she spoke. "Dr. Woods wanted to have a quick look to make sure she was stable enough to be moved, but they said no, no, we will take her right now, our ambulance is on the way. They wouldn't even let Dr. Woods near her. That doctor who came said he would give her a thorough exam and would assume responsibility for her well being. Her husband signed her out, AMA, but that was about it. Their ambulance got here a few minutes later, they loaded her up and they were gone."

"That's an interesting story. Why would someone do that, do you suppose?" Zach asked, his interest piqued.

"That's what we were wondering. Dr. Woods said there had to be something fishy going on there, for them to not even want him to make sure there was no internal bleeding, or brain hemorrhage, or anything like that," Lydia said, still animated.

"Pretty weird, for sure," Zach said, his thoughts spinning. "Don't suppose there's any way to get the name of the doctor who signed her out? Though I'm guessing I know who it is."

"That's not privileged information, I think I can find that pretty easily," Lydia said, hoisting her ample self off of a surprisingly small chair. She waddled over to a cart loaded with hanging files, shuffled through them quickly and pulled one out. "Here we are, a doctor Raymond Mathias, general practitioner."

"I thought as much. Except he lost he license several years ago, and is no longer practicing medicine. Not legally, at least," Zach told the woman. "Why would someone allow their wife to be taken from a hospital to be cared for by a discredited doctor, without even letting a real doctor have a good look at her first?"

"Well now, your guess is as good as mine on that." Lydia gave a deep chuckle. "We were all more than a little puzzled by it, but he claimed to be a doctor and can legally do that. I mean he could, if he was still legally a doctor. No one thought to verify the man's credentials. It all happened so fast. And her husband was right here, signing her out, so the hospital's hands were tied."

"You don't know the half of this story, this is not the oddest thing to happen to this woman by a long shot. Including the fact that the man who signed her out was a complete stranger to her, only posing as her husband," Zach decided to drop that bomb and see her reaction.

"Whaaaat?? He wasn't her husband? He had her ID, his ID, all the right things," she began to babble.

"Oh don't worry, you did nothing wrong, it was all part of some elaborate plot of his, and he did his homework well. He almost had her convinced that she WAS his wife." Zach assured.

"Well don't that beat all?!" she said as she sank back into her chair. Zach couldn't help but watch it sag in protest as her full weight was deposited onto it.

"Yeah, no kidding. Oh, one more thing, how did he and his doctor friend get here so soon after the accident? I can't figure that out, they were here almost as soon as she was brought in, weren't they?" Zach had to ask.

"From what I understood of the whole thing, they were in the car right behind her. The phony husband guy said he was trying to catch up to her. She left their house in such a rush she forgot something, he said. Guy never hear of a cell phone?" Lydia shook her head in disgust.

"Oh really. That was pretty convenient, wasn't it?" Zach said thoughtfully, "I really appreciate you talking to me."

"You are welcome! You figure out what that man's game is and stop him, would you?" Lydia said waving a finger at him.

"I'll do my best," he smiled as he left, with yet another baffling piece of the puzzle.

Chapter 11

As he left the hospital, Zach mulled over this new information. Elise not only had a discredited doctor caring for her concussion, but she had never even been seen by a bonafide doctor after the accident. Why didn't Harold want the ER doctor to have a look at her? Was he afraid of what the doctor would find? Or what he wouldn't find. He needed to talk to the EMTs that responded to the accident that night. Next stop, Waukesha fire and rescue.

The guys at the fire station were friendly and talkative, much to Zach's delight. Several of them remembered the call Zach asked about. Harold must have left quite an impression on them, and it wasn't a good one.

"When we got to the scene, this character was already there, pulling the woman out of the car. When we told him to let us move her, he went berserk! Said it was his wife and he could move her if he wanted to," a young muscular EMT said, shaking his head. "When we told him she needs to be placed on a back board and her head stabilized, he said she wasn't hurt that bad."

"And how would he know that? He was a real ass, said they already called their own ambulance! Who the hell does that?" one of the first responders chimed in.

"That is pretty weird, I never heard of that," Zach had to agree. "So then what, you guys loaded her up and took her?"

"We sure did, we weren't going to leave her there with him. He called us every name in the book while we loaded her up, said he was going to sue each of us, the station, the county, you name it. We just drove off, and him and the skinny guy with him got in their car and followed us," the EMT said. "There was no sign of their ambulance until we got to the hospital."

"So did any of you get a chance to look her over on the way there? Was she conscious? Any obvious injuries?" Zach asked.

"She was in and out of it, must have gotten a good hit to the head, but was able to answer a few simple questions before the lights went out. She also tried to get up until we restrained her a little more securely. But no, we didn't really get a chance to check out her injuries, just kept her stable until we got her to the hospital." A third guy piped up.

"What did you ask her?" Zach was curious.

"Easy stuff, what her name was, did she know what happened, the date," one of the men explained.

"Anybody happen to remember what she said her name was?" Zach could feel his blood pressure rising.

"It was Elsie, or Lizzy, something like that."

"Elise maybe?" Zach offered.

"Yeah, that was it, Elise. Do you know how she is now? Sure has a jerk for a husband," the first guy commented.

"Actually she's doing pretty good. She's why I'm here, that guy who gave you all the grief wasn't even her husband. Just pretending to be, and I've been hired to try and figure out why." Zach told them as he climbed back into his truck, then thought of one more thing.

"The guy who hit her car, was he treated at all?"

"No, it was a young kid in an old pickup truck. He refused medical treatment, cooperated with the two cops who were on the scene, talked to the guy who was supposedly the husband, and he left. His truck was damaged in the front, but drivable," one of the older guys told Zach. "Funny thing was, now that I think of it, he acted nervous, like he wanted to get out of there ASAP, but he didn't act shook up like people usually are after hitting someone. More like how someone acts when they're lying and worried about getting caught at it."

"I assume the police got his name? I would love to talk to him," Zach said.

"They must have, they took down all his info before letting him go."

Zach made his second trip to the Delafield police department and was fortunate enough to bump into Officer Lang again. Since she knew the whole story about Elise already, it was a quick procedure to get the accident report from her. It took all of about five minutes to get the name and address of the other driver and be on his way. Office Lang wished him luck and asked him to keep her informed. He immediately drove to Milwaukee, to 37th and National Avenue, a less than spectacular neighborhood, and found Danny McArthur's address. It was the upper half of an older, but cared for, duplex. Seeing that it was the middle of the day, Zach didn't figure he'd have much luck getting ahold of Danny, but it didn't cost anything to try. He rang the bell, then knocked on the door to the upper a few times with no results. He knocked once more, then started to leave, when the second door on the porch, belonging to the lower flat, opened.

"You looking for Danny?" He's a good boy," said a lumpy

middle aged woman with several plastic curlers in her graying hair, a cigarette hanging out of the corner of her mouth and the most solid unibrow Zach had ever seen.

"Yes, I am looking for Danny, but I don't think he's done anything wrong," Zach said, trying to look friendly and harmless. "I just need to talk to him about an accident a few weeks ago."

"He don't know about any accident, he's a good boy," she repeated, folding her arms across her more than ample chest. "And he ain't home anyway. He's on vacation."

"That's too bad, I'm from the insurance company and I have a check for him," Zach said, thinking quickly. "I'll just take it back to the office and tell my boss he isn't available, and I'll check back next time I'm in the neighborhood. Thanks for your help," he said as he started to step off the porch.

"Wait! A check? Oh that accident, the one where he dented his truck?" she said, her memory suddenly improved. "I can take that check for him and give it to him when he comes back."

"Sorry, can't do that. He has to sign a few papers, then I have to give it to the person named on the check, a Daniel McArthur. You can tell him I was here, and I'll be back in this area again in a couple weeks."

"He's my nephew, my sister's boy. He's the good one. He just had a little fender bender, that's all," she said, "he could sure use that check money."

"Where is he on vacation? If it's in my district I can catch up with him and give it to him, otherwise it goes back to the office. You'd be amazed at the number of unclaimed checks we have there," Zach said as he rubbed the back of his head.

"Well, I guess he won't mind if I tell you, he's between jobs right now, and likes to hang out at that pizza place over on Forest

Home. You know, the one with all the pool tables? He'll be there playing pool with anyone who'll play with him." She said as she took a big drag off the cigarette then crushed it onto the wooden floor of the porch.

"Thanks a lot ma'am, I'll see if I can catch up with him over there," Zach smiled at her, "Forest Home and what?"

"Bout 43rd or 44th, can't miss it, big ugly green awnings," she said as she stepped back inside her doorway and shut the door.

It was a very short drive to the pizza place. The narrow buildings were practically on top of each other, mostly brick, most with awnings and all looking like their latest renovations occurred ometime in the 1960s. Danny's aunt was right about the pool and pizza place, the oversize awnings were big, old, and a really nasty shade of pea green. Zach stepped inside the small establishment, where the owners apparently didn't know there were laws against smoking indoors. The air was so heavy with smoke it was difficult to make out the people inside. Zach coughed a few times and stepped into the haze, looking for the pool tables. They were in the back of course, where the smoke was the thickest. The smell was a mixture of cigarettes, cigars, beer and body odor. He tried not to breathe any more than necessary.

There was a young guy at the pool table, playing with an older man who looked like he could be the kid's grandfather. There were two crumpled, worn five dollar bills resting on the edge of the table as the two men played their game. Zach leaned back on the counter, ordered a diet Coke, and watched quietly until the game ended and the young kid snatched up the two fives.

"You Danny?" Zach asked.

"Who wants to know?" the kid asked as he stuffed the money in his jeans pocket and pulled a cigarette from the pack he kept folded into his tee shirt sleeve. His dark hair was slicked straight back, with a few loose strands falling onto his forehead. He looked like someone out of 1950's bad boy movie.

"Name's Zach," Zach said, still leaning on the bar. "I'm looking for anyone who knows anything about an accident that happened a few weeks ago."

There was a slight twitch to the kid's head, but otherwise no reaction. "What makes you think I can help you with that?" He asked as he set the balls up for another game.

"Because your truck was involved in the accident." Zach stated, "don't worry, I'm not a cop or anything. Just need a little information."

"What kind of information? I told the police what happened, I ran the stop sign and hit the lady's car. Got a ticket, paid a fine and my insurance has to pay for the broad's car and medical bills," Danny said, playing with a few of the balls in his hand. "What else is there?"

"Yeah, I read the police report, but I need to know the stuff you didn't tell the cops. The way it really happened," Zach said, trying to read the guy.

"I don't know what you're talking about." The kid said as he quickly scanned the room, as if looking for Zach's accomplices.

"Hey, you don't want to say anything, that's fine, this is just a courtesy call, really. Thought I might give you a chance to distance yourself from old Harold before he is officially charged." Zach shrugged, daring to hope the kid would take the bait.

"Charged? With what?" Suddenly Danny lost all his bravado and looked like a scared kid that's just been caught with his hand in the cookie jar.

"Okay, first off, I'm not after you, I'm after Harold. I want to make that clear. I'm not a cop and anything you tell me goes no further, got that?" Zach told Danny, who looked ready to bolt out the door.

"Yeah, sure, okay." Danny's color came back to him and he sat on the stool near Zach. "He told me I wasn't breaking any laws, just ensuring a positive outcome, is what he said."

"What exactly did he have you do? Wait for a specific car and hit it on purpose?" Zach pressed, his hunch seemingly correct.

"Well sort of, but her car wasn't moving when I hit it. I met him out there on that empty road, he got out of the car the lady was in, and he parked it right in the middle of the street. Then he told me to back up, get up a little speed and run into it, so it looked like I ran the stop sign." Danny explained, talking softly, as if reliving the event. "He promised me she wouldn't be hurt, she was drunk, he said, and he wanted to scare her into not driving drunk anymore. Is she okay? I didn't really hurt her, did I?"

"No, no, she's okay. She's why I'm here. I'm trying to figure out why Harold did that to her," Zach reassured him. "Where did he find you?"

"I told you why he did it. He said his wife drank too much and sometimes drove after drinking too much. He wanted to scare her into thinking she was so drunk she got in an accident and didn't even remember it. Hell, that would scare me," Danny repeated, "he called me, said if I did this for him, he'd see that my brother's legal bill would go away. He's my brother's lawyer, and my mom was going to mortgage her house to pay him, and if I did this, she wouldn't have to. My brother's kind of wild, robbed a used car lot, but there were cameras in the place, so he was ID'ed. His legal fees were going to bury my mom, but she was going to do it anyway. So I did it for her."

"Thanks for telling me this, Danny, I appreciate it a lot. This gets me a little closer to figuring out this whole sneaky deal."

"That's okay, it felt kind of good to get it off my chest," Danny admitted. "I'm glad his wife is okay."

"Thing is, that wasn't his wife, and she wasn't drunk. My guess is, she was drugged by him or his buddy. I hate to say this, but unless your brother is going to trial really soon, he may need to find a new lawyer," Zach told him as he stood to go. "I don't have the whole thing figured out yet, but when I do, I'm pretty sure Harold's going to be on the other side of the table in a courtroom." Zach nodded and left, with Danny standing there, mouth wide open.

Chapter 12

Things were starting to come together. It looked like the whole thing was an elaborate plan to nab Elise and claim she was his wife, Melody. But why? What had happened to the real Melody, who was obviously lying in Dr. Mathias' basement in a comatose state? And why did he need to replace her? Which brought back the question of who was the woman that died in the apartment fire? At first Zach figured that had to be Melody, but that apparently wasn't the case. His head hurt from all the confusing details. He was still missing a few important pieces of the puzzle. He decided to take a break and let all this new information settle for a while. He'd run over to Franklin and talk to Alvin Hooper about his phantom intruder.

Alvin was home, puttering on something in his garage, when Zach drove up.

"Afternoon, Mr. Hooper," Zach said pleasantly as he walked up.

"I wondered when I was going to see you again," Alvin said, wiping his soiled hands on his pants before shaking Zach's hand.

"I didn't want to show up until I had some answers for you," Zach said, "and I have them now." He explained how him and

Bastian had put the motion sensor field camera up and aimed it at his balcony for several days.

"So you got photo evidence? That's great!" Alvin said, his face animated. "Can the guy be arrested, even though he didn't make it inside?"

"Well, yes, I have photo evidence, but no, he isn't going to be arrested." Zach couldn't help but smile a little, "it was a tom cat." He opened his iPad and showed Alvin several of the shots he had of the perp on his balcony.

"What? A cat?" Alvin was incredulous. "A damn cat was trying to break into my place?"

"No, I don't think he was trying to break in, he was just being a cat. Your balcony is out of the wind, near some pretty big trees, so it's an easy one to get onto. He just sat a few places, had a look around, got startled when he knocked over your pots, and left. End of mystery." Zach explained with a grin.

Alvin wasn't as amused. "So how do I keep him off my balcony? He's going to keep knocking my stuff all over the place," he sputtered.

"I'm not too sure how you'd do that, you'd have to ask animal control I guess," Zach shook his head, and ran his fingers through his unruly hair. "Or leave him some cat food on your balcony and make friends with him."

"What!? I don't need a damn cat friend. Next thing he'd want to do is come inside my place, and then what?" Alvin said, disdain evident in his voice.

"Just a thought," Zach suggested, "you know what they say, keep your friends close, and your enemies closer."

Yeah, I heard that. That cat isn't a friend or an enemy. Just a nuisance. But thanks for clearing up the mystery for me," Alvin muttered. "Not as exciting as I would have liked, but at least no one is trying to break in the place. Maybe I should get a dog. He'd keep the cats and burglars away!"

"Not a terrible idea there. I've got a young one myself and he's my best buddy," Zach agreed. That taken care of, he headed back to his office.

Kelly had some very good news for him, on a personal level. He had asked her earlier to look into finding him someplace to live, closer to the office, that also accepted large dogs. She was pretty sure she found him the ideal location.

"You know who Jim Lempke is, right? The guy who owns this whole building?" Kelly began to explain her good news to Zach.

"Sure, of course, the landlord. Nice old guy. Not raising our rent is he?" Zach asked with a smile.

"No, you signed a lease, remember? Since he's lived in the area forever, I asked him if he knew of any places around here that take large dogs, and are for rent for a single guy. He said he knew of one place you might be interested in. The apartment upstairs!" Kelly said with a big grin.

"Upstairs? Right here? With Rudy?" Zach asked incredulous.

"Yup! How perfect is that? You already know the fenced lot in back is fine for Rudy, and Mr. Lempke said he knows you and Rudy so he's not worried about renting to you at all. The place will be empty the end of next month, so it's yours if you want it."

"That is better than I could have dreamed! Can't get much closer than right upstairs. Kelly, what would I do without you?" Zach gave her a big happy grin.

"You will never know, Mr. Marchand," she said with an equally happy smile.

"Will you please stop calling me mister? You make me sound

as old as Jim Lempke," Zach said, not for the first time.

"I've called you Mr. Marchand since I was sixteen. It's a little hard to stop now."

"Try it, just say Zach," you can do it, he coaxed her jokingly.

"Zach…." She said, shaking her head with a smile.

"See? Easy. I'm Zach. My father is Mr. Marchand," Zach said as he gestured with his hands. "Thanks again for finding such a perfect place for me. Please tell Mr. Lempke I would love to take the place. I'll give my notice tonight. Did he mention any particulars, like price, or how many bedrooms it has?"

"You don't think I'd drop a pearl like this on you without all the details, do you? It's two bedrooms, plus a small alcove off the living room, an actual dining room, one bathroom, and your own laundry. He said you can have it for $700 a month. There are four apartments upstairs, each about the same size as the businesses below. Since your apartment would be directly above us here, it would make it about 1200 square feet. How's that for particulars?" Kelly told him, "oh one more thing, your next door neighbors are those two old sisters who bake bread all the time and sell it at the farmer's market, so it probably smells great up there."

"That all sounds perfect. Two bedrooms, so I can have one for Nathan. He'll love that. Now that he's eight, I'm sure he has some definite ideas on what he'd like in a room. Other than a bed for Rudy that is. He sure loves that dog," Zach said, still smiling, "you're the best Kelly."

With Kelly's news putting him in a great mood, Zach could only hope the rest of his day would go half as well.

*   *   *   *   *

With a lot of help from Zach and Bastian, Elise was able to start putting her life back together. For now, she was staying with Bastian, who loved the company, but her old apartment would be ready for her in another day or two and she was anxious to get settled into it. She drove around, reconnecting with her clients, and setting up new training schedules with them. As she drove to the Wilson home, where they had two lively young labs, Elise suddenly remembered something. The Coffee Cup, a coffee and bakery shop she used to love! On a whim, she decided to stop there. As she was walking through the door, enjoying the delicious smells wafting out, she remembered something else - bumping into Harold here! That's why she vaguely remembered him. She had coffee with him here at least once. She struggled to pull the memories to the surface. Why would she have coffee with him? Did she know him? Then it came to her, he had grabbed her arm and whirled her around, knocking her purse to the ground. Then he instantly had apologized, saying he had mistook her for his wife, and had insisted on buying her a cup of coffee to apologize. She also remembered their brief conversation, about his wife checking up on him, even though his visit to some woman named Liz was purely business. He had made several comments about how much she looked like his wife, which after two or three times, made Elise a little uneasy. Knowing what she knew now, her instincts about him were correct.

Forgetting about fresh coffee, delicious bear claw pastries and dog training, Elise walked across the street to the old brownstone building she remembered Harold gesturing toward, whenever he was saying Liz wasn't a girlfriend. Why he had bothered to ramble on and on to her, as complete stranger, she didn't know. Knowing all she did about Harold now, she highly doubted that Liz was just a client. Why didn't she come to his office, and not him come down to the east side of Milwaukee to meet with her?

The outer door of the older building wasn't locked, so Elise let herself in and found the mailbox wall. She looked for a Liz, or Elizabeth on any of the mailbox fronts, but most people only had last names. She gave a frustrated sigh and started to leave.

"Looking for someone?" A young man asked as he prepared to exit the building with his 10 speed.

"Yes, my friend Liz lives here, but she didn't tell me her apartment number," Elise said lamely.

"Liz, Liz, oh Lizzy Ashford, yeah, 3B, but she's not home. Been gone a few weeks now. Better try calling her to see when she'll be back," he told her as he hopped on his bike and rode it right out the door.

Not home for a few weeks? Bells went off in Elise's head and she knew it was time to call Zach. She did, and told him all she knew. He agreed it was something that needed a closer look, but he didn't want her going any further with it. He told her to go on to her dog training, and he'd see what he could find out.

It didn't take Zach long to get to the address Elise had given him. Like her, he was able to walk right into the lobby. He walked up to the third floor, and it was easy to spot 3B instantly, by the pile of newspapers by her door. He knocked, knowing there would be no answer, and he tried the door. Then he went in search of the building manager.

"My sister hasn't answered my emails or phone calls for a couple weeks," he told the manager in apartment 1A. "And I see there's a lot of papers piled by her door. We need to get in there and make sure she's not hurt or something."

"Well, we don't normally do that," the skinny guy who answered the door replied, "I mean, isn't that invasion of privacy or something?"

"Not if you think she might be in need of help," Zach said. "She never misses Sunday dinner with our folks, and she's missed two now. We're really worried about her. I guess I could call the police, and they'd come, and you'd have all sorts of questions to answer and forms to fill out."

"Ahh, I guess we should have a look. But I'm coming with you, got that?" the manager told Zach.

"Of course, I'd expect you to," Zach smiled.

They went up to Liz's apartment, Zach picked up all the papers lying there and the manager unlocked the door. He could tell as soon as they stepped inside, it had that deserted smell to it. Zach moved quickly through the place. There was food molding in the fridge, a few dirty dishes in the sink, and a layer of dust on everything. No one had been in there for awhile. Zach noticed the blinking light on the answering machine. He looked away and continued to check the rooms for any clues. Her purse was on her dresser, her wallet and cell phone still inside. She had two empty suitcases in her bedroom closet, and it looked like all her clothes were still there.

"Look, are you going to be much longer?" Manager man asked impatiently.

"A little longer, I can let myself out. I'm not taking anything, honest," Zach said with a smile.

"Yeah, okay, just be sure you lock the place when you leave. And don't take nothing of hers." He left and his footsteps could be heard down the hall and down the stairs.

Zach quickly turned his attention to the answering machine. It had a number of messages on it. Most were junk, but several were from the same guy, someone named Greg. He was pretty persistent and sounded like he was probably a good friend. Zach decided to give him a call, from Liz's phone. Greg picked up on the first ring.

"Lizzy! Where the hell have you been? I been calling and calling!" came the frantic voice on the other end.

"Sorry Greg, but this isn't Lizzy. I'm calling from her apartment though. Are you a friend of hers?" Zach asked pleasantly.

"I am, who wants to know? Where is she? What's happened to her?" Greg asked, panic evident in his voice.

"Names Zach, I'm an investigator. She seems to be connected to a case I'm working on, and I have no idea where she is. Can we meet and have a talk?"

"Sure thing! I'm five minutes from there - meet me at the coffee place across the street. I'll be wearing a Packers hat," Greg said and promptly hung up the phone.

Zach took one last quick look around and left, making sure to lock the door behind him. Greg was already standing outside the coffee shop when he got down there.

"Thanks for meeting me. I wish I had more information I could tell you about your friend, but I just got here a few minutes ago myself," Zach told Greg as they went inside and ordered cold drinks.

"Damn, she hasn't answered my calls for about three weeks, and that's not like her! We touch bases a few times a week, you know, to cry on each other's shoulders," Greg said shaking his head. "I'll tell you what though, if anything happened to her, I'd bet money her loser married boyfriend had something to do with it!"

"Loser boyfriend? You know him?" Zach asked.

"I never met the guy, but I know he's married. Name's Harold something. She's always talking about him. Harold got me this, Harold got me that. She's not his girlfriend, she's his mistress. I told her that and she went ballistic! No, he loves me, she says. No, he don't, he's using her, and paying for what he gets with trinkets." Greg was fuming as he spoke about Harold. "I told her to get rid of him and get a decent boyfriend. Someone who will take you places besides your bedroom."

"Doesn't sound like a great guy. In fact, I've met him and he isn't. The more I learn about him, the less I like him," Zach said slowly. "I sure wish I knew what his game was."

"What game? He's married, with a mistress on the side. Not a real original game." Greg said.

"No, that's just the tip of the iceberg, he's got himself in the middle of something, and I'm trying to figure out what it is." Zach gave Greg a brief version of everything that was going on, and waited to see his reaction.

"Holy shit! Are you kidding me?" was all Greg could manage to spit out. "I don't get it."

"You and me both. I'm guessing there's a connection with your friend Liz and all this other stuff going on too. It all seems to be connected somehow. Hell, if this was Criminal Intent, I'd have the whole thing solved in under an hour!" Zach laughed ruefully, referring to one of his favorite TV shows.

"Well all I can tell you is I haven't heard from her for at least three weeks. Last time I talked to her in fact, I was pretty pissed at her. She was letting old Harold call the shots again, even though she wasn't thrilled with his latest request," Greg said through gritted teeth.

"What request? What did he want?" Zach asked, unprepared for the answer.

"He wanted her to get a tattoo to remember him by, can you believe that? Remember him by? He's a sugar daddy, not someone she's going to want to remember ten years from now." Greg said, still seething.

"A tattoo? That is pretty odd. Hopefully not his name in a heart!"

"Hell no! He wanted her to get a damn dog tattoo on her ankle! What the hell is that for? He didn't sound like any dog lover to me!" Greg spat out.

Chapter 13

With a sinking feeling in his stomach, Zach knew he had just found another piece to the puzzle. The woman who died in the apartment fire was Liz.

"Aww, shit man, I hate to have to tell you this, but I think I know what happened to your friend," Zach said sadly. "She could be the one who died in the apartment fire I told you about. The tattoo was all they used to ID the body. I'm really sorry."

"Oh hell, Lizzy, no…." Greg gulped. "Are you sure it's her?"

"Like I said, she was ID'd by her tattoo. They're probably going to have to exhume the body and test for DNA." Zach sadly explained, "I'm really sorry."

"I knew that son of a bitch was no good for her!" Greg's sadness turned quickly to anger, "why didn't she listen to me when I told her to get rid of him? Why did she have to agree to that damn tattoo?"

"That guy seems to be no good for anyone. I could be wrong about your friend, but she's been missing the right amount of time, and that damn tattoo is pretty unique," Zach said. "I only wish I knew what the hell all of this was for? One woman is dead, another in a coma and a third was kidnapped and passed off as his wife. How in the hell are they connected? Why? Who else can I talk to?"

"Hell, as shitty as this is finding out about Lizzy like this, I don't envy you at all. It doesn't make any sense to me," Greg said, shaking his head. "Do you think his wife in a coma is what started all of this? Did he need someone he could pass off as his wife for some reason? I can't think of any reason he couldn't tell people his wife was in a coma, instead of trying to find a stranger to be her! That's just sick."

"I sure wish I could get my hands on that guy's cell phone and find out who he's been talking to the last few weeks. I think it's time I called a cop friend of mine." Zach muttered more to himself than to Greg. They talked a bit more and parted ways. Zach promised he'd let Greg know when the burn victim was identified. He got back to his truck and immediately called Ron Scolari, his homicide detective buddy.

"Homicide, Scolari," came the crisp, always the same, comment.

"Hey buddy, how's it going?" Zach asked warmly.

"Marchand you old dog, what are you up to these days? Ever solve that mystery of the lady with two names?" Scolari laughed, remembering the confused woman he spoke to several weeks earlier.

"I'm still working on that case, which is why I'm calling. It got even more complicated, and I think there's a murder involved." Zach started. He got Scolari up to speed on everything he knew, and ended with his suspicion about Liz being the burn victim in the apartment fire. If that was the case, the fire was arson and she was murdered.

"Jesus, Marchand, don't you ever do any simple cases, like find runaway kids or cheating husbands?" Scolari said, knowing Zach lived for the complicated cases. "So this possible victim lived over on Farwell Street, but the fire was in Waukesha? Guess we need to find out where she died. All right, I can take this from here, and get the Waukesha guys involved when I need them. I'll keep you informed."

*   *   *   *   *

Harold's fury was evident to everyone in the room. "I don't care what you have to do or how you do it, but you find her and get her back here. And soon!" he snarled.

"We're trying, we'll get her, don't worry," a thickly built, street thug sort of guy said confidently. "She's going to turn up by herself someplace, we only missed her by half an hour this morning."

"And Ray, you going to have to figure out what dose to use on her, and get it right this time, dammit! I can't afford to turn her into a vegetable too," he directed his frustration at Dr. Mathias. "Do you people realize what's at stake here? Millions of dollars. Millions. You'll all be set for life if you don't screw up. I need her here and acting like she's my wife before Memorial Day or the whole thing falls apart. Am I making myself clear?"

There were four men in the room that he directed his rage at. Dr. Mathias was one, Eli the street thug was another, plus a shady looking mafia wannabe who went by the name of Mad Mike, for his habit of flying off the handle with little or no provocation. The fourth was a Jamaican man, known only by the name Flame, for his expertise in setting fires. He stood with his arms crossed, leaning on the door jamb, amused by Harold's outburst. Flame knew that hysteria wasn't needed to get the point across, calm and cool always worked better.

Harold wasn't used to dealing with criminals as people he needed something from and paying them for it. He was used to them needing his skills as a criminal attorney, and them paying him. He much preferred having the upper hand, rather than trying to get these lowlifes to do as he asked.

"Cool your jets man, we will find her. We know her old routine, and she's getting back into it," Mad Mike said, sort of bouncing as he talked, "we just have to figure out where she's living now, but we will."

"Well you better, I'm not dishing out this kind of money for a bunch of screw ups," Harold said, his anger finally dissipating. He ushered them out of his office, sat back in his large leather chair, and straightened his necktie. He hated losing control like that, but sometimes he couldn't help himself. He had to count on others to get her back and he didn't like the uncertainty of it. He couldn't keep telling his family, and his father especially, that Melody had a slight relapse and was hospitalized again. Sooner or later they were going to get suspicious. No visitors, he told them, was what the doctor thought was best for now. Another couple days was about all he had. And he knew it. But for now, like it or not, he had to back off, let those lowlifes do what he was paying them to do, and he needed to concentrate on his work. He was due back in court.

*   *   *   *   *

Zach met up with Elise and Bastian at their apartment building. Elise was finally getting her apartment back, and new furnishings were being delivered. She was excited to be getting her own place again, but a little nervous about being alone. She felt like someone was watching her all the time. It was an unsettling feeling, and hard to brush off. Besides, with Harold out there, who knew what else he was up to?

Zach told them about his meeting with Greg, and finding out all he did about Liz. That included the fact that Harold had her get the same tattoo Elise had. Immediately they both knew this unfortunate Liz was the woman who died in the apartment fire. It was also obvious it wasn't an accident.

"How did they get her into my apartment, and me out, without me knowing it? I mean, all I remember is being at home that evening, my pizza was delivered, and the next thing I know, I'm being pulled out of a strange car after the accident." Elise asked, something she hadn't even thought of until now.

"I was working that evening, so I don't know if anything weird went on around here," Bastian commented.

"You ordered pizza, and that's the last thing you remembered?" Zach asked, his interest piqued.

"I ordered it, and it was delivered. I remember answering the door, with money in my hand, and the pizza guy stepping in, and that's it. Don't remember him leaving, me eating the pizza, nothing," Elise explained, trying to remember anything else.

"What pizza? A chain? Did he have a uniform on?" Zach asked.

"No uniform, it's from Moe's down the street. Just a small mom and pop place. I've gotten their pizza before. The guy was just wearing regular clothes, with a Moe's baseball cap. Nice guys always though. Why, what are you getting at?" Elise looked at him, tipping her head.

"I think I'd like to go talk to the folks over at Moe's," Zach said with a quick smile, "wonder if any of their delivery guys can be bought off?"

Zach left the two of them there to wait for furniture deliveries, and strolled down the street to Moe's Pizzeria. He chatted up the woman taking orders, and ordered a pizza to go. She was middle aged and friendly, probably the owner's wife, Zach guessed.

"I've heard great things about your pizza," Zach told her with a smile, "have to try it for myself. Do you deliver too?"

"Yes, we do, Marco, my son does most deliveries, or Guilio, my nephew. They deliver quickly, so your pizza is still hot!" she proudly pointed out.

"Are either of them here? I'd like to talk to them if I could," Zach said, still smiling.

"Guilio is doing deliveries right now. Marco is in back, cutting up fresh ingredients," she said, then turned and yelled into the back of the shop. "Marco, come up here! Gentleman wants to talk to you!"

Almost immediately, a young man appeared, wiping his hands on his apron. He was clean cut, looked to be about twenty years old or so, and very friendly. "Hello, I'm Marco, how can I help you?"

"I'm trying to find out who delivered a pizza to a friend of mine, about three, almost four weeks ago," Zach said.

"Geez, that's pretty hard to remember, where do they live?" Marco said, furrowing his brow.

"Over on Buckley, big apartment building," Zach offered. "I think she gets a delivery every month or so."

Marco shrugged. "We deliver to those buildings almost every day. Anything different about her order that we'd remember?"

"Well, I'm not sure, but I think whoever delivered it, was paid off by someone to let them deliver it for them. Does that sound like something you remember?" Zach asked, knowing it was an

NOT MY LIFE 121

incredibly long shot.

A blank look crossed Marco's face, then he lit up. "Hey, I bet I know when that might have been. It was Guilio's delivery, probably a month ago. He came back without his hat after a couple deliveries, and my mom read him the riot act for losing the hat. She docked his pay twenty bucks to pay for a new one. He said that was cool, because some dude paid him fifty bucks to let him have the hat and deliver the pizza for him. So he was still up thirty bucks. He should be back anytime."

"That would be the night I'm talking about," Zach said. Just then, a skinny, olive skinned kid entered the small shop, wearing a red Moe's cap, and carrying an insulated pizza bag. "You must be Guilio."

"Yeah, I am, so what?" The kid said, without much interest.

"I need some information about the night you let a guy deliver a pizza for you," Zach said, trying to sound official.

"What are you, a cop?" Guilio asked defiantly.

"No, I'm investigating a murder at that apartment that night. Do you want to talk to me here, or shall I call my cop buddies?" Zach asked softly.

"Hell no. I didn't do nothing wrong. Guy said his girlfriend lived in the apartment. Even knew her name and apartment number. Said he wanted to surprise her and deliver her pizza. Gave me fifty bucks and asked for my cap." Guilio shrugged. "I thought it was a pretty cool thing for him to do, surprise her like that."

"Did you happen to see the news the following day about a woman who died in that same apartment that night, when a fire was started there?" Zach asked, looking intently at the scrawny kid.

"Holy crap no, I didn't know that," he said as the color left his face. "I didn't do anything...."

"I didn't think so. But I need to know if you remember what the guy looks like who gave you the fifty bucks." Zach told him.

"Just a regular white guy. Kind of muscular, kind of short, hair combed straight back. Had on a muscle shirt with some sort of picture on it," Guilio thought for a moment, "oh yeah, he had tattoos on his knuckles, E, L, I and a star. I asked him what ELI stood for, and he said his name was Eli, and the star was what people will be seeing when they connect with his fist."

"That's real good, you remembered more than most people do. Anything else? Did you see a car or anything?" Zach praised the kid.

"No, no car, but I think he might have been with another guy, who was standing across the street, leaning in a doorway, watching us. He was really dark skinned, and tall, and wild red and yellow hair, like flames sort of. He didn't look too friendly," Guilio said.

"Thanks a lot Guilio, you might be helping us stop a really bad guy. The police will probably be coming to talk to you in the next day or two, be sure and tell them everything you told me," Zach said as he paid for his pizza and left.

Back at Elise's apartment, Zach found her and Bastian moving furniture around. When he came in with a fresh hot pizza, their urge to move heavy furniture disappeared. As they ate, Zach told them what he learned from Guilio.

"Wow, so you think this Eli guy came in and drugged me or what?" Elise asked, wide eyed.

"Or chloroformed you, or even gave you a good knock in the head. Just enough to get you out of the building quickly and quietly and put Liz in there in your place," Zach surmised.

"But why put Liz in there? Why not grab me and leave the apartment empty?" Elise asked.

"Because you have people that would come looking for you, Liz doesn't. She has a couple close friends, but even they weren't really looking for her, just calling her house every few days. After almost a month, none of them thought to go to her apartment to even see if she was lying in there, dead. I'm guessing Harold knew she wouldn't be missed, and you would be. So with your family and friends thinking you died in your apartment, he was free to mold you into the replacement for his comatose wife." Zach explained his theory, "only thing I don't know, is why he needed a stand in for his wife?"

"From what I heard in that basement, the coma she's in was their doing. So that means before she was in that coma, she was alive and well, and they did that to her to make her forget her current life." Elise said.

"But she already was his wife. There was nothing for her to forget, or was there?" Bastian said. "Maybe she was not the compliant, loving wife he wanted, so he was going to erase her mind and give her only the memories he wanted her to have? That's pretty far fetched. Why not divorce her and marry someone more to his liking?"

"That's it! Maybe she wanted a divorce and he didn't. But that's still not a reason to do what he did. Either figure out your problems together, or get the divorce, and move on," Elise said, "and why did he say he needs me pregnant?"

"There has to be more. Some reason why he has to have his beloved, loving wife Melody, by his side. Melody wasn't cooperating, so he needed someone who would. But why? What could it possibly be? It had to be something pretty major to go to these measures, even killing a woman," Zach racked his brain. "He also had to have the help of at least one unscrupulous doctor. Did this Dr. Mathias guy actually do your plastic surgery too?"

"Wait, I almost forgot. Harold kept saying something about things need to happen before his father's meeting, whatever that is," Elise suddenly remembered.

Chapter 14

"That could be it! Elise, you might have just handed us the missing piece," Zach said excitedly, as Elise and Bastian stared blankly at him.

"What? You know about his father's meeting? What it is it? And why would his wife have to be there and broadcasting that she wanted to start a family?" Bastian asked with a deep frown on his face.

"I have no idea what this meeting is, but I'm sure as hell going to find out! Don't you see? Everything must be culminating with this meeting. It ties everything together. It's got to. I need to figure out how to get a meeting arranged with Harold's dad." Zach's eyes glistened with excitement. He was close now and he knew it. And a phone call a few minutes later confirmed some of his suspicions.

"Zach, it's Scolari. Thought you'd want to know, we exhumed the body from the apartment fire and compared the DNA to hair fibers found in the apartment where Liz lived. No surprise, it's a match," Scolari said without bothering with a greeting. "Got anything else for me?"

"More suspicions, that's about all right now. Don't suppose you can look up a person by his tattoos, can you?" Zach asked.

"More tattoos? Not another person with the same one?" Scolari groaned.

"No, how about a street punk with ELI and a star on his knuckles. His name is Eli, but I don't have a last name," Zach told him.

"That's a long shot, but I can give it a try, got anything else on him?"

"Unfortunately no, but I'm pretty sure him and a guy with wild red and yellow hair were the ones who took Elise from her apartment and put Liz there, and started the fire. Hopefully she was already dead when they set the fire," Zach told him, then added, "and you probably want to send someone to talk to a kid named Guilio at Moe's pizza, down the street from Elise's apartment. He's the one who gave me that info. And you might want to have a talk with Harold Richardson, as he is the one who got Liz that tattoo, shortly before she disappeared."

Zach filled Scolari in on a few more details and went back to his office to see about getting a meeting with the senior Mr. Richardson. Elise was going to see one of her dog clients, and Bastian was going to wait at her apartment for one last furniture delivery.

Elise drove to the south side of Milwaukee, where Marge, a middle aged woman lived with her two German Shepherds. One she had owned since it was a pup, but the other was a very large, three year old rescue from a local pound. Rex had been scheduled to be put down, as being too aggressive for adoption, but Marge knew better. This was fear, not aggression she was seeing. She took him home a few months ago, and her initial impression of him had been correct. He was calming down, learning to trust her, and becoming a wonderful companion. There was no sign of aggression. She did need some help with some of his training though, like heeling and coming when called. She was glad Elise was back and able to continue her work with him. Elise came, and took Rex. She walked him down the street to a dog friendly park, working with his heeling as they went. She noticed someone behind them, almost half a block back, that seemed to be keeping the same pace as she was. She stopped abruptly and turned to go toward the park. The guy she thought was following her, kept going, his attention on the music in his headphones or the cell phone in his hand. She gave a quiet sigh of relief, and continued to the park. She was getting paranoid, she thought. She turned her attention to the park. She was glad to see it was empty, so she could work with Rex without any issues. She sat Rex, praised him for listening, then released him to run off so she could work on his coming when called. She had a thin lead about forty feet long on him, to give him room to run. As soon as Rex took off, she stooped down to call him back, when she was shoved to the ground by someone from behind.

Too late she realized it was the guy who had been following her! She struggled with him for a few seconds, but he was young and very strong. He shoved her head to the ground, and was about to push a cloth into her face, when out of nowhere, Rex appeared. In the blink of an eye, he had knocked the guy to the ground and stood over him, snarling and barking. Elise scrambled to her feet and pulled her phone out of her pocket. With shaking hands she called 911, then Zach. The guy struggled to get up, but Rex didn't allow him to move. He snarled within inches of the guy's face, spattering him with his slobber. Elise unhooked the long lead from Rex's collar and wrapped it around the guy's legs a number of times. He wasn't going anywhere in a hurry.

Police arrived quickly and took over. As fast as Rex had turned into an attack dog, he calmed down, all smiles and wagging his tail.

"That's a heck of a dog you have there, he'd be great for police work," one of the officers said as he escorted the shaken up guy to the squad car.

"I agree, he would be. But he's not my dog, I'm just training him for someone else," Elise said as she gave Rex a much deserved neck scratching. When you get this guy to the police station, there's a detective named Ron Scolari, in homicide, you need to call. Tell him you just picked up a guy with E L I tattoos on his knuckles, he's looking for him."

After taking Rex back home, and telling Marge about his exciting morning, Elise went back to her apartment and told Bastian what had just happened.

"Oh my God, I knew I shouldn't have let you go alone! He could have grabbed you!" Bastian gasped, giving her a long hug.

"But he didn't, thanks to Rex. I need a dog like that," Elise said with a big smile, then added, "but then, when the guy was squirming on the ground and Rex wouldn't let him up, I saw the tattoos on his knuckles. It was that Eli guy!"

Just then Zach arrived, all out of breath from running up four flights of stairs. "Are you all right?" he huffed, catching his breath. "You went out alone?"

"I'm fine, and Rex was impressive!" Elise said happily, "and Eli is in police custody. Hopefully your friend Scolari will talk to him soon and get something out of him."

"That was really good you noticed the tattoos, or he would have been released within the hour," Zach said. "I hope the guy is ready to talk. He might be part of something a lot bigger than he bargained for."

Just then Zach got a phone call he had been waiting for, from Ernest Richardson's office. Ernest would be available for a brief meeting with Zach the following morning. Zach was hopeful he'd get some answers there. Enough answers to put all the pieces together and make sense of Harold's activities. With Bastian promising to keep a close eye on Elise, and go with her if she went anywhere, and Elise promising to stay home when Bastian went to work, Zach was comfortable leaving them and getting back to his office.

Kelly had some new cases for him to look into when he got back, so he made a few phone calls and set up appointments to meet with potential new clients. The last call was to a Mrs. Ramirez. Her voice sounded familiar, but he wasn't sure.

"Mrs. Ramirez, aren't you the cook at the Richardson home?"

"Yes, yes I am! That's why I call you, you seem to be a nice man, when Melody was having her trouble," she said, sounding a little out of breath, "but please, call me Marjorie."

"You remember that Melody wasn't really her at all when I came out to help her, don't you? That was Elise," Zach said, completely baffled by her comments.

"Yes, that's what you said, and then she disappeared! I am not sure who she was. She is gone. If the woman you say you helped was not Melody, where is Melody?" the woman said, sounding confusing and confused.

"I think I have an idea where she is, but is that why you're calling me, to ask where the real Melody is?"

"Oh, no, no. I'm calling you because my Raphael told me he thinks Harold, Mr. R, is up to no good. He told me he saw Mr. R. carry a woman out of here that night, when Melody disappear. Later he tells us she got sick and went back to the hospital. We wondered about that, she didn't seem sick, and why would she need to go back to a hospital with no visitors and no phone calls for two weeks? We hear Mr. R talking to his family on the phone, and he gets very mad when they ask why they can't go see her. Now Raphael tells me he saw four men coming out of Mr. R's office yesterday, all together. He knew one was the Doctor who was caring for Melody, but the other three are evil he said. He knows one of them, Mad Mike he called him, who will do anything for anyone, if the price is right. Raphael didn't let any of them see him. After they all left, he went in to see Mr. R with a package he needed from the house. Raphael told Mr. R he didn't know he had Mad Mike for a client, you know, just making conversation. He said Mr. R got very mad at him and told him to mind his own business. He said whoever he thought he saw leaving the office, he was mistaken, and if he knew what was good for him, he'd keep his thoughts to himself," Marjorie said, sounding out of breath yet.

"What do you know about this Mad Mike? Did Raphael say anything more about him?" Zach asked, realizing he was probably part of the crew Harold had hired to do his dirty work.

"No, he only told me that Mad Make was bad news, from the old neighborhood, when Raphael was a rough street kid. I know he knew lots of bad people, and he never wanted to be like them. He wanted out of that life, for good," Marjorie explained.

"Where is Raphael now, can I talk to him?" Zach asked, wanting a little more info on this Mad Mike, and possibly the others he saw with him.

"That's why I call you! I can't find my Raphael! He come home for lunch yesterday and told me about what happened at Mr. R's office that morning. Then he go back to work for the day, and now I can't find him! He didn't come home last night, he never does that.

He doesn't answer his cell phone, and his truck is gone. I call the police but they say I can't file a report on him for three days! So I call you, Mr. M, you are a good honest man. I think you can find my Raphael for me," Marjorie said, finally expelling a large breath.

"So you're saying the last time you saw him was at lunch yesterday? Did he say where he was going or what he was doing that afternoon?" Zach didn't like where this was heading.

"I see him in the yard in the afternoon, pulling weeds. Then he leave in his truck. That's all, he don't come home for dinner, and he don't come home all night. My Raphael doesn't do that. He never misses any dinners and he calls if he's going to be even a little bit late." Marjorie said firmly.

"And his truck is gone, his cell phone too I imagine? Anything else?" Zach asked.

"No, what else? No nothing, just him and his truck, and he keeps his phone in his pocket all the time," she asked, alarm evident in her voice.

Zach hated to ask her, but he had to. "Did you look in your closet? Any clothes missing, anything like that? His personal belongings?"

"No, no, he didn't even come into the house. He was out weeding, got a phone call, got in his truck and leave. I saw him go. I'm in the kitchen. I even wave to him at the window, but he didn't see me," she said sadly. "I can pay you Mr. M. We don't have a lot of money, but we have a little saved up."

"Don't worry about that, Marjorie, I think this might all be connected to Melody's disappearance somehow and everything else that's going on," Zach told her, realizing that currently he had no one paying for this mess, but he had to see it through to the end.

He was in too deep to walk away now. Nobody ever said he was going to get rich in this business.

Chapter 15

The following morning, bright and early, Zach took a ride to the law offices of Richardson and Heath, though from his understanding, Heath had been bought out by Ernest Richardson years ago. He quickly surveyed the area, took notice of a row of carefully pruned shrubs in a row next to the walkway as you approached the firm's front doors, and attached his motion sensor camera in amongst the thick branches. He knew this little camera could come in handy, and this seemed like a good way to get some of Harold's cohorts on film. Once he was sure it wasn't visible to passersby, he went up the walkway for his meeting. It was a very attractive grey brick building, sort of modernistic, but in a classy way. The guy had good taste in architecture, he'd give him that. The tasteful design carried inside the building as well. The lobby was spacious without being grand. Clean pale marble floors and large windows were evident in all directions, with a round receptionist desk in the middle. The receptionist was middle aged, efficient and friendly, spoke Zach's name into a phone system and quickly pointed him to an office down the hall. So far, Zach was more impressed with

Ernest than he was with his son, and he hadn't even met the guy yet.

He gave a quick knock on the door and was promptly invited to come in. Ernest met him halfway across the room, welcomed him with a firm handshake and invited him to sit down. The room was tastefully furnished in leather and chrome. Not too much of either. There were numerous photos on one wall, of Ernest with various city officials, senators and sports figures. The guy had connections. After a quick survey of the room, Zach studied the man before him. Like his son Harold, Ernest was tall and fit, but the father carried himself proudly, where Harold almost seemed to slump in comparison. Ernest had shockingly white hair, but a thick headful of it. His beard was white as well, short and neatly trimmed. He had alert, piercing blue eyes, that had a smile in them. In spite of his son, Zach instantly liked this man.

"What can I do for you, Mr. Marchand?" Ernest said in a strong, booming voice, as he offered a cup of coffee to Zach.

"Please call me Zach, Mr. Richardson," he said, not sure where to begin. He didn't want to alienate him right off the bat. "I'm not sure what you can tell me, if anything, or how much I should be telling you. I'm at a bit of a dead end in my investigation, and I'm hoping you can open a new door or two for me."

"First of all, let's keep this informal, my name is Ernest. My father was Mr. Richardson. I'm not old enough for that title yet," the elder man chuckled. "What sort of an investigation? You said on the phone that you're a private investigator? Who or what are you investigating? What might this have to do with me, or my law firm?"

Zach took a deep breath, and started. "It has to do with your son, Harold. He's been involved in some less than ethical activities lately, and they all seem to culminate with a big meeting or something that you are having around the end of the month. Do you know what he's referring to?"

"What sort of unethical activities are you speaking of? He's a very good attorney, and if any of his cases can be overturned by his actions, I'd like to know about them sooner, rather than later." Ernest said, appearing unruffled by this news. "As for my activities for the end of the month, it's common knowledge here I am making a company announcement at my Memorial Day party. There's a lot of speculation among my attorneys, and my family, regarding what I'm going to be informing everyone of. I can't tell you exactly what my announcement will be, but I can say it is regarding my reduced involvement in the firm, and someone making named partner. I am 72 years old and am ready to step down, Zach. I can only do that when I am comfortable with the continued stability of this firm. We have 14 attorneys here, including two of my sons, Harold and his younger brother Thomas. Both are associates here, with hopes of becoming equity partners one day. I tell you all of this so you can understand what is probably going on in Harold's mind."

"Thank you for being so frank, Ernest, I appreciate that. So Harold is probably thinking he's going to move up the corporate ladder. That isn't enough of a motive to explain his rash actions," Zach said, shaking his head. "Could there be something more? Something he thinks could be happening?"

"If you told me what he's been up to, perhaps I can shed a bit more light on this," Ernest said, then paused and added, "providing nothing said here leaves this room, why don't we both lay all our cards on the table?"

"All right. This is going to sound a little far fetched, but hear me out," Zach said as he pressed his palms together in front of his mouth and took a long pause. "This all starts with his wife, Melody."

"Wait, before you start, do you know where he has taken her? He said her condition deteriorated after her accident and she needed to be re-hospitalized. But he says she can't have visitors or phones calls, no flowers, cards, nothing. What is going on with her? Do you know?" Ernest said, leaning forward in his chair, his interest piqued.

"Well, unfortunately, I know a lot about what is going on with her, and she's the reason I'm here. Let me explain. This might take a while," Zach said, glancing at the clock on the wall, and silencing his cell phone. He wasn't sure if it was a good or bad idea to be so frank with the father of the man he was investigating, but Ernest seemed to be a man of good scruples.

Ernest held up one finger, then leaned over to his intercom, hit a button and told Helen to reschedule his appointments to clear his entire morning. Then he motioned for Zach to continue. So he did. He began with the phone call he received from Elise, when she still wasn't sure who she was. He explained her gradual return of her memories, and Harold's insistence that they were figments of her imagination. He told Ernest about Elise being kept in the doctor's basement, along with a comatose Melody, all she overheard down there, and how she escaped. He told him about the fire in Elise's apartment and the woman who died there, and her relationship to Harold. Zach told Ernest about Eli's near miss trying to nab Elise again, Eli's arrest, and the eventual police involvement in the investigation. Last he told him about what Raphael had seen and told his wife about, and his disappearance that afternoon. Then he sat back and waited for a response from the older man.

Ernest let out a long low breath. "That is a hell of a story," he said at last. He leaned back in his chair, obviously digesting all he had just heard. "I don't know what to say, I can't believe my son would go to these extremes to get what he wants, but it actually explains a lot. Especially about Melody. So you say the real Melody is lying in a coma in some doctor's basement? Why on earth would he do that? That's his wife, for God sake. Can't someone get her out of there? And what of that poor woman he abducted? Where is she? What is she doing?"

"The police have been given all this information, and if they haven't gotten Melody out of there yet, it will happen soon. Elise is doing well, putting her life back together, but apparently Harold has some thugs out there still trying to get their hands on her. Harold will be picked up soon, for questioning if nothing else at this point. But we need motive. Why would he do all of this, just to have what appeared to be his wife, at his side, for your party? And telling people she was anxious to start a family at last? Why not just bring the real Melody to the party?" Zach asked.

"I think I have a good part of the answer," Ernest said, thoughtfully. "Harold is very goal oriented in his thinking. Things have to be just so for him. It's well known that I maintain tight reins on my family, including my grown children. I don't approve of all the divorces and remarriages that are so common these days and my children know this. I expect two people to marry for life, raise their children together, and work through any rough times together. That's what a marriage is. Those vows are taken far too lightly these days, and I don't approve of it in my family. I also want a grandson to carry on my name. I don't make a secret of the fact that I'd like my firstborn son to have a son of his own to carry on the family tradition and name here. Harold has two daughters from a previous marriage. He has no contact with them as they grow up, which I wholeheartedly do not approve of. He knows this has done him a great disservice in my eyes, not only regarding his placement here, but his inheritance when I leave this earth. He also knows if he can manage to hang onto his current marriage and produce a son it will have a great impact on his standing with me. I will not abide by another divorce on his part. He will be left out of my will entirely. My son Thomas has a teenage daughter, who is a delight, but she is not a male to carry on the name. My daughter has a charming six year old son, but she is no longer a Richardson, nor is he. So you see, this leaves the door wide open for Harold, if he and Melody were to have a son, in the near future."

"Ok, this all makes sense to some degree, but why do they have to have a son in the near future? As long as Harold and Melody stay married, you're happy, and if a son comes along in the next few years, you'd be even happier. So why the sudden rush? Why does he think this all has to fall into place in a matter of weeks?" Zach asked, stilled puzzled.

"Because I don't have a few years to wait, Zachary, I have a year left, at best," Ernest stated simply. "I am dying of cancer. My family is aware of the situation. I don't want or need sympathy from them or anyone else. That's just the way it is. You play the cards you are dealt. But I want to know there is a male heir on the way, or born, before I die, for he will inherit the bulk of my estate, which is considerable. We are not just talking a few million, we are talking billions, with a B. The others will all walk away with a few million, so no one is entirely left out. But an infant boy will get the brunt of my fortune. If that boy is Harold's son, Harold would of course have control of the money as the boy grows to adulthood and proves himself. To Harold, this would be as good as him getting the money himself. He has tried to talk Melody into having a child for the last several years, but she really doesn't want one, or possibly can't even have one, I don't know. But they've been married for almost eight years and have no children yet. So to produce a new Melody, not a new wife, who is pregnant, would be quite a feather in Harold's cap and he knows it."

"Wow, now it all makes sense, doesn't it?" Zach said with a soft whistle. "It all boils down to money. He'll kill, maim, kidnap and drug whoever he has to, to get what he wants. Incredible."

"I told you he was goal oriented. He just seems to have taken it a bit too far," Ernest said, shaking his head slightly. "I thought he has been preoccupied with something lately. He hasn't been as focused on his cases as he usually is. Now I understand why. I do appreciate you telling me all of this, though I'm sure I'd be hearing it from the police in due time anyway. Nice to have it all explained in one neat package."

"I appreciate your frankness as well. This has filled in a lot of the missing holes for me," Zach said.

"Though I can't say I condone his methods, I must say I admire my son's ingenuity, going to all this trouble to create a new improved version of his current wife. I don't know if I would have ever thought of something like that myself." Ernest chuckled wryly, then asked, "have the police picked up my son yet? Sounds like he's going to need a good lawyer, though, what exactly can he be charged with at this point, do you know?"

"Well, I'm sure they'll be able to tie him to Liz, the woman who died in the fire, so that's murder, for one. Kidnapping Elise would be two, whatever he did to Melody to put her in a coma, would be three I'm guessing," Zach stated, counting the charges off on his fingers, "plus, he hired someone to set the fire, so that's arson, hired someone else to hit the car with Elise in it, and fake the accident, I'm not sure what that's called, but the list seems to go on and on.”

“I suppose so, but it's assuming the police can connect all the dots, like you did. If not, they're a bunch of random acts, most of which can't even be connected to him without a witness or proof of some sort. I don't believe he's in quite as deep as you think,” Ernest said with the hint of a smile.

“What are you talking about? Did you hear everything I told you?” Zach said, not believing what he was hearing. “Everything is connected back to him. All the people in one way or another, and all the crimes. He could easily go away for life, no matter how good a lawyer you are.”

“But you aren't hearing me, Zachary. You connected all the dots. The police haven't. They can bring Harold in for questioning and he will have a reasonable explanation for every question they throw at him, believe me. But at the end of the day, they won't have anything they can hold him on, and he'll be released. Mark my words, he'll come out of this okay, and will achieve his goal one way or another.” Ernest said calmly, without emotion. “Now you, Zachary, are the only real obstacle for him, because you have connected all the dots, and you do know who the critical witnesses are, and where any evidence can be found. So the question now is, what do we do with you, Zachary?”

Chapter 16

Zach didn't know what to say. He was astonished. "I don't get it, what are you going to do, get rid of me, so no one else can put all the pieces together and come to the same conclusions I did? What about all the people I told you about, Elise, her friend Bastian, Eli who was picked up this morning, Marjorie, her husband Raphael, the list goes on and on, are you going to get rid of all of them too? Just to protect your son?"

"Ha ha, hardly Zachary, this is not to protect my son, this is to protect my firm, my legacy! Do you realize what a scandal like this would do to my firm, and all the people who work here? We would be ostracized in the legal community! Would people hire us as their trusted attorneys after something like this made headlines everywhere? I think not," Ernest said in a cold controlled voice as he leaned forward in his chair, elbows resting on the desk in front of him. "Everything I've worked for all my life would be gone. I'd have money yes, but the legacy would end, and not only end, but be destroyed. Tainted. I cannot and will not allow that. And no, I don't need to have all those people you mentioned killed, that would draw too much attention. I'm not a stupid man. I need to make only two of you disappear, and the rest will shut up tighter than a basket of clams, and disappear on their own. Most will be happy to be paid off and go on with their lives, a little richer, and none the worse for wear."

"You can't really think you'll get away with this, do you? Don't you think people will wonder where I am when no one can find me?" Zach asked, anger evident in his voice.

"Please, don't flatter yourself. You could have met up with any sort of mishap, a car accident, home fire, heart attack, bomb in your office, who knows," the older man explained with a smile. "If I thought you could be bought off, I would have offered to set you up for life, but we both know you wouldn't have considered it for even a minute. I took the liberty of looking into your life after you called yesterday for an appointment. Virtue above all else. Save the people, make a difference. How noble. How pathetic. You aren't even getting paid for this case, and yet you plod deeper and deeper into it, until you stand ready to ruin my entire empire, for nothing. You can't bring back that girl who died in the fire, or make Melody whole again, so what will you accomplish, beyond putting Harold in jail, and ruining me? And I haven't done anything wrong! Don't you see this flaw in your thinking? You end up punishing the wrong man."

Zach sat speechless, staring at the cold grey eyes looking back at him. Slowly he stood. "So now what?"

"Well, I'm sorry to say, this is the end for you. I have enjoyed our little visit, but it's time to part ways." Ernest stood up as well, and shrugged. "You know though, one thing puzzles me. You seem like a pretty smart guy. Did you think you could just march in here, get me to tell you whatever it is you wanted to know, and I would happily lay it all in your lap? Just like that? To help you ruin me, my firm and my eldest son? Are you really that naive?"

"In a perfect world, I guess that would have happened," Zach said flatly.

"I can't let you just walk out of here, you know. You'll ruin everything. Our little conversation won't be repeated to anyone." Ernest said, sounding regretful.

"Like I said, in a perfect world, I would have gotten all I needed from you, and you would have been unhappy to help put your own son behind bars, but you'd also know there are laws against killing people, kidnapping, arson and all the rest. And no one, not even the son of the upstanding Ernest Richardson, is above the law," Zach said as he took a step closer to the desk. "But this isn't a perfect world, and you're right, I'm not that naive." He opened his shirt to reveal a thin wire taped to his chest.

"You son of a bitch! You're wearing a wire!" Ernest roared, his face turning beet red as he scrambled around the desk. He was fast and strong for a man his age. But Zach was faster and stronger. He grabbed the older man, spun him around and twisted his arm around to his back, leaning him over his desk. As he did so, several policemen burst into the office, from where they had been sitting outside in their van, listening to and taping the entire conversation. They led Ernest out in handcuffs, with a smug sneer on his face. Zach stood there for a moment to collect himself. Shaking his head, he exhaled deeply and left without another word to anyone.

He drove directly to the Delafield police station, and found Officer Patricia Lang, who helped him set up the trap for Ernest to walk into. He told her the whole thing had gone better than he thought it would, but they still didn't have Harold.

"Well, we haven't been just sitting here enjoying the scenery while you do all the work. We picked him up an hour ago, he's in interrogation right now," Patricia told him.

"Getting anywhere with that yet?" Zach asked, hopeful.

"Not yet, he's denying pretty much anything we don't have solid proof for, which unfortunately, is almost everything."

"What can you get him for?" Zach asked, not liking the sound of this.

"So far, not a whole lot. Regarding the accident, he said he took Elise to a private hospital and paid her medical bills and all, because he met her a few weeks earlier, and recognized her at the accident, where he just happened to be right behind her. He said he knew she didn't have health insurance, so thought he'd do a good deed. Said she was totally confused about him saying she was his wife. He was only trying to help her. He claims she got mixed up, because he told the people at the hospital he was her husband so they'd let him take her. Said she was free to leave his house any time she wanted to, and we could ask his hired help if we didn't believe him," Patricia sighed. "We're working on that right now, but it doesn't look good."

"What about the girl, Liz, who died in the fire? Did he admit to anything with her?" Zach asked glumly.

"He said, yes, he knew her, and they did have an off and on relationship. He asked her to get that tattoo of the dog because he saw it on Elise and thought it was cute, that's all. Had no idea how she got into Elise's apartment or how the fire was started, nothing." Patricia continued, "his prints are of course all over her apartment, but he readily admits to being there. So unless someone steps forward and says he paid them to put her there and start the fire, we have nothing."

"What about that Eli guy, the one who attacked Elise in the park? He was the one who delivered the pizza to her place and got into her apartment," Zach suggested, "he had to have been paid to do that by Harold."

"Most likely, but he isn't talking either, according to your buddy in homicide. He insists it was just a joke to deliver the pizza to her, and when he attacked her in the park, he didn't even know it was the same person. He was just trying to rob her. So they have him for a mugging, that's about it. Says he never heard of Harold."

"Damn it! How do we get something with teeth in it, to nail him?" Zach asked, totally frustrated.

"We're working on it. We've got squads going over to that doctor's house in Hartland, to pick him up for questioning, and get the comatose woman out of his basement. We have another car at Harold's house, talking to the hired help. That's about it for now, anything you can add to it?" she asked.

"I wish. This is going just like his father said it would. Harold would have an answer for everything, and he'd be back on the street in an hour. No one, aside from Elise, is saying anything against him, and he has an equally wild story to counter hers, so it's he said, she said," Zach grumbled. "Damn it."

Patricia paused their conversation to answer her phone. She motioned for Zach to stay where he was. She listened for a few minutes and hung up. "You aren't going to want to hear this, but there isn't a lot we can hold his father for either. He doesn't condone his son's actions, but it doesn't sound like he knew anything about them beforehand. And he said you might meet with an accident of some sort, but that's at best a threat. Other than that, all he told you is he's dying and wants to find a suitable successor to take his place in the firm."

"Shit, I was afraid of that. So they both get released, get back to their lives, and Elise has to worry about when she's going to be nabbed off the street and turned into a zombie wife?" Zach asked.

"Do you think now that Ernest knows Harold's plan to do that, he'd still bother doing it? What's the point? He'd know it wasn't the real Melody," Patricia pointed out.

"He would, but no one else would, so to the rest of the family and firm, he kept to his convictions of cutting Harold out of the will if he divorces again. It's all about appearances for that man," Zach said, a plan forming in his mind. With Harold busy in the interrogation room for at least another hour, Zach made a quick run to his house to talk to Marjorie. As he suspected, she was reluctant to speak with him.

"Marjorie, did Harold tell you not to talk to me or the police?" he asked as she tried to close the door on him.

"Please go away, Mr. M., or I will never see Raphael again!" she said, barely keeping it together.

"I can find him for you, I promise, and bring him home," Zach told her, "but I need your help. He's an evil man doing a lot of evil things, and we need to stop him and put him in jail where he belongs."

"How can you bring Raphael home? How do I know I can trust you?" she said hesitantly.

"Have I ever lied to you? I'm not lying now," Zach coaxed her, "Harold needs you to keep quiet about how he made you all think Elise really was Melody. Once that lie is exposed, his whole story collapses."

"What do you want me to do? The police were already here and I told them just what Mr. R. told me to say. That Elise was here, to recuperate from her accident, she was just a friend, and free to leave anytime." Marjorie said, as if she had memorized it.

"I need you to tell me a little more about the family. What

about Edward, the youngest son? No one ever mentions him. And what about Melody, does she have any family?" Zach asked her.

Immediately, Marjorie relaxed. This was not the sort of thing she thought Zach was going to ask her, and she was visibly relieved. And happy to talk. She ushered him into the kitchen.

"Edward is the black sheep of the family. He has no interest in being a lawyer, and is not, how do you say, materialistic, like the rest of the family. There was a falling out when he did not want to go to lawyer school. He moved away years ago, and he is not mentioned. But I do know the sister, Virginia, does keep in touch with him once in a while. I heard her discussing it with Thomas one day. Not in a bad way, just saying no one needed to know. And for Melody, her parents die a long time ago. She has a sister, in Iowa I think. That's all." Once Marjorie started talking there was no stopping her. Zach got the most current information she had on Edward and Melody's sister Cecelia. He thanked her, promised again to bring Raphael home safely, and left, telling her not to say anything of his visit to anyone.

It didn't take long for Zach to track down Edward Richardson, who was living in Portland Oregon. At first, he was reluctant to talk to Zach, and almost hung up the phone. But Zach was able to calm him down enough to get him to listen to him. He gave Edward a very brief rundown of events, and then came right out with what he needed to know.

"Unless I can find someone, or some way to connect all these crimes, your brother is going to go scott free. And your father isn't going to do anything to help me, obviously," Zach explained to the man who preferred to be called Eddy.

"I'm not surprised by what you've told me, Harold always was a chip off the old block. Do whatever you want, no matter who you hurt in the process. The end justifies the means," Eddy said, sadness evident in his voice. "I don't know what you want from me though, I've been out of touch with both of them for probably a decade."

"Does your father have a weakness in his armor? Something that would make him turn on Harold?" Zach asked.

"Boy, I doubt that. Not the prodigal son. Even after everything you told him Harold did, the first thing he wants to do is brush it all under the carpet so it doesn't taint the firm. He's all about image and that damn firm. We grew up with it lorded over us. Give him a grandson to carry on his name, follow in his footsteps, blah, blah, blah. Who needs to hear this when you're fourteen or fifteen years old? Harold wanted to hear it, that's for sure." Once Edward opened up to Zach, it was like the dam breaking. Zach knew to be quiet and let him talk. "Did you know the reason Harold divorced his first wife? Because she gave birth to two daughters! Can you believe that? She didn't give him a son, so he dumped her and shut all three of them out of his life completely. What kind of guy does that? He was determined to have the son he needed to get his hands on our father's money. Much to his relief, Thomas had only one child, a girl, and although our sister Virginia, had a son, he's not a Richardson. So all Harold needed to do was remarry, and have a son. Can you imagine how crazy he must be by now, eight years later and still no kids with Melody? I keep in touch with Virginia, so I know all of this. She's not 'heir to the throne' so we can talk freely."

"Sounds like some seriously screwed up family dynamics. I'm sorry for you," Zach said sincerely.

"Hey, don't be, I'm fine. I'm happy. I've got a nice job as a middle school teacher, happily married to a great gal, and we have two great kids. And here's the funny part. I have a son, Adam. He's almost five. A Richardson boy. Doesn't that beat all?" Eddy laughed heartily, "and old dad doesn't have a clue. But back to your problem. The only thing I can think of that you might try, is to talk to my brother Thomas. He's also an associate at the firm. You might be able to convince him it would be in his best interests to get Harold out of there. Not exactly sure how you can do that, but he's not the same mindset as Harold and old dad. He can actually be reasonable."

"Thanks for your help, Eddy, you've given me hope if nothing else," Zach said.

"Hey, glad I could give you something," Edward replied. "And if it comes up in conversation that old Ernest already has a grand-son, I don't care. You might be able to use that tidbit as salt to rub in a wound."

"I'll try and keep that information to myself, and only use it as a last resort, but thanks," Zach said. He hung up the phone and sat quietly for a while, pondering his next move. He didn't have to ponder long - his cell phone in his pocket rang.

Chapter 17

Zach pulled out the phone. It was Bastian. "Hey, what's up? I was planning on stopping over there later this afternoon," Zach greeted him.

"It's Elise. We need your help, like right now," Bastian said quickly.

"Oh shit, not again, what happened? I'm on my way, keep talking." Zach groaned as he jumped up and ran out of his office to his truck.

"I'm not at home. I'm following a van on I-94, going south. Elise is in it," Bastian said.

"They managed to get to her? How? Didn't you stay close to her?" Zach said, irritated.

"Yeah, of course I did, but this morning, she was moaning about having to worry every time she stepped out of the house, that someone was going to grab her. I told her I'd stay with her, but she said she wasn't going to live like that any longer. She said she had a plan, and she was going to do it with or without my help, so obviously, I had to help her. We tried calling you a couple times, but it went to voice mail. Anyway, she used herself as bait, went out to a couple of the little markets down behind Main street this morning, hoping one of Harold's goons would be lurking nearby to grab her. I went along too, but not right near her. Just close enough to keep her in sight. I stayed parked in my car, about half a block away. And sure enough, I see some guy in a pin stripe suit watching her, following her, not too close. He's looking around to make sure she's alone, and I could tell he was waiting for her to walk further down the block, away from all the people at that farmer's market," Bastian explained. "She knew it too, and walked down a dead end alley between a couple buildings, and he followed her. A minute later, he comes back out, half carrying her, like she's walking drunk. Puts her in his van and took off."

"Are you kidding me? You let her do this? Now they have her and you don't know where he's taking her?" Zach said through clenched teeth as he pushed down on the gas pedal a little harder.

"She was going to do it whether I followed her or not, so what was I supposed to do, lock her in a closet? I haven't lost her, I see the van ahead of me, and we both installed an app called Footprints on our phones, so I can follow her in real time, even if I'd lose track of the van. But I won't. So just hurry up and get caught up to me, he's driving really slow in the right lane. I'm guessing he doesn't want to risk a ticket," Bastian told him, his nervous voice not sounding as confident as his words.

"All right, all right, I am coming, but I'm half an hour away at best. How far are you?" Zach grumbled.

"Just coming up on Seven Mile Road. We're in luck, there's a lot of construction up ahead, so everyone is slowing way down," Bastian said.

"For once, I'm happy to hear there's road construction somewhere," Zach muttered. "Just don't lose sight of that van. Anything distinctive about it?"

"Uh, not really, it's white, probably ten year old Ford Econo-van. It's got some company name on the sides and back, a carpet cleaning service I think. Didn't get a chance to get a good look at it," Bastian replied. "Want me to get closer to it and see what it says?"

"No, just follow it. How is that app working?"

"Looks like it's working perfect. A little red dot on my screen shows exactly where she is on the map, and it keeps moving, up ahead of me."

"I still can't believe she did this, what does she think it will accomplish by getting picked up and hauled off someplace?" Zach said, irritation still obvious in his voice.

"She can't live like this, Zach, not free to go anywhere, always wondering if she's going to be grabbed," Bastian said softly. "She wants to force things to a head, that's all."

"And what if they take her somewhere, fill her full of drugs and she ends up like Melody?"

"They won't do that, Harold wants to make her into his wife, remember? Hey, hold on, we are leaving the interstate, getting off on highway KR, know where that is?" Bastian said.

"Yup, I'm catching up to you, only about ten minutes from there," Zach said as he stepped up his speed a little more.

"Ok, he's going east on KR, but there's not a lot of traffic, so I'm hanging back pretty far," Bastian told him.

Zach went as fast as he dared, without getting stopped for speeding. He was thankful whoever grabbed Elise was driving insanely slow. He got to KR, and headed east.

"We just turned left, on 90th street, and he's going really slow. Turning into an old farmyard. I just drove right past it so he didn't know I was following him," Bastian said, starting to sound pretty nervous. "Are you getting close yet?"

"I am, I just crossed H, so I'm close to 90th, where are you?" Zach replied, making a point of keeping his voice calm.

"I went past the farm house about a mile or so, there's an intersection, Braun Road, I'm turning around here and waiting for you."

"Got it, I'll be there in just a couple minutes!" Zach said, no longer concerned about speeding tickets. He sped up, turned left on 90th street and roared down the road to the intersection where Bastian was waiting. Bastian jumped out of his car as Zach approached, and hopped in the truck before it had time to stop.

"Okay, go slow, it isn't far," Bastian said, relieved to have Zach back in the driver's seat, in more ways than one. "There it is, right before those pine trees, on the right."

Zach wasn't sure what they'd do once they got here, but he figured he'd think of something. He turned onto the gravel drive-way, crawling slowly, looking for the van. "I don't see a white van, are you sure this is the right place?" Zach asked.

"Yeah, this is the place, keep going, the driveway looks like it goes around the house to the back," Bastian pointed.

Zach inched past the old colorless farmhouse, following the gravel path as it gave way to more and more grass and less gravel. Behind the house two old pickup trucks were parked, but no van. There was a barn about a hundred feet from the house, and another small building. Zach pulled in and parked next to the two old trucks. "I think we better walk from here," he told Bastian.

They ran to the barn, where the door was wide open. It was filled with normal barn contents, some machinery, bales of hay, but no van. They hurried around the back of the barn to a smaller farm building. It looked like a steel storage shed of some sort. With a still warm, white van parked next to it. Zach motioned for Bastian to come closer to him.

"I'm guessing Elise is in here, but we don't know how many people are in there with her. Rather than running in with guns blazing, I'm going to try and reason with them," Zach said quietly to Bastian.

"Good plan, since we don't have a bunch of guns to do that blazing thing," Bastian nodded.

Zach walked up to the closest door and pounded on it a few times, loud and firm. He waited, then pounded on it again. Nothing. He tried the door, and was surprised to find it unlocked. With more guts than brains, he decided to barge right in, with Bastian close on his heels. The building was basically empty, except for a few stacks of drywall and some hand tools. It looked similar to the inside of an unfinished basement, with the framework and insulation all in place, and a few sheets of drywall nailed up. In the far corner of the building were three doors, to rooms that looked like they were small offices or bathrooms. Zach headed to them. The first door opened to reveal a bathroom, clean and looking freshly installed. The next room was unfinished, with bare drywall on the walls and a roll of carpet leaning in the corner. The third door was locked. The room looked to be about the same size as the other two. Zach rattled the doorknob again.

"Anyone in there?" He called, hoping to get an answer. "Elise? Are you in there? It's Zach and Bastian."

The two men listened for a response, but got none.

"Did you hear anything?" Bastian asked.

Zach shook his head. "Hello, anyone in there, make some noise if you can."

"Did you hear that?" Bastian said, "sounded like a thump or something, I think."

"I'm going to break the door down," Zach said, backing up for some leverage. He rammed into it with his shoulder, hearing wood crack as he did. He gave a second go at it, and the wood splintered and gave way. Zach stumbled into the dark little room. A muffled call came from the corner. Bastian found the light switch and turned it on. There in the corner, tightly tied and gagged, they discovered Raphael. But no Elise.

Chapter 18

"What the hell?" Zach muttered as he rushed over to the man lying in the corner. "Where is Elise? Was Elise here, Raphael?"

Raphael shook his head as he struggled to sit up. Zach untied the gag around his mouth. "No, two men were here for only a few minutes. They let me use the restroom, then tie me back up. No one else in here," he said, sounding scared.

"Bastian, get him freed and take him to my truck, I'm going up to the house," Zach said, a sudden coldness in his voice.

"Are you sure that's safe?" Bastian asked.

"I don't care. This has gone far enough. You two wait for me in the truck." He strode quickly out of the building and up to the house. He pounded loudly on the back door. He waited only a few seconds and was ready to pound on it again, when it opened.

A small woman opened the door. She looked worn out, tired and scared. Her faded clothes hung on her rail thin body. She didn't say anything or make any move to stop him as Zach pushed the door wide open and walked inside. "Where is she?"

The scared woman pointed to the stairs in the next room. She watched, void of any emotion, as he walked past her and climbed the stairs two at a time. Upstairs, there were three rooms, he stuck his head in the first to find an empty bedroom, with an unmade bed and a fat cat lying in the middle of it. As he went to open the second door, a man was just coming out of that room.

"Who the hell are you?" the man asked? He was dressed almost comically, like a gangster from Al Capone's days, with a pinstripe suit and wingtip shoes. The only thing missing was the fedora.

"I'm Zach. Came to get Elise and take her home. Who the hell are you?" Zach said standing firm as if he belonged there and pinstripe was the intruder.

"Name's Mike. Mad Mike, to most. And you aren't taking anyone, anywhere," he crossed his arms, spread his legs and stood blocking the doorway.

"Look Mike, I don't know what your game is, but we're all done playing. I know Elise is here, we saw you bring her just a few minutes ago. She's coming with me. We can do this the easy way, or I can just shoot you and take her. Your choice." Zach said with a cold smile, as he moved his jacket aside to reveal his 357 at his side.

Mad Mike paled a little at the sight of the gun, and his stance weakened, but he tried to hide his discomfort. "Like I said, she's not going nowhere."

"Suit yourself. Want to close your eyes, or what?" Zach asked as he slowly pulled his gun out.

"Wait, wait, no shit, you'd shoot me? You'd really shoot me?" Mike said, holding his hands up in front of him. "I didn't sign up for getting shot at."

"Hell yes, I'll shoot you, and your skinny, spaced out friend in the kitchen too, if I have to. I'm taking Elise home. Anyone gets in my way, they get the same treatment," Zach said, knowing full well he had no intention of shooting anyone. "Now get Elise and bring her out here."

Mike went back in the room he was blocking, and returned with Elise. She was unharmed, with her wrists tied in front of her. He quickly fumbled with the cord and untied them. "There. Here she is, take her and get out of here."

"Oh not so fast. We're going to have a little talk first, Mad Mike. Me and you, and your buddy who's lurking around, and your skinny friend in the kitchen. We're all going to sit down and have a little talk. Got that?" Zach said, pointing his gun at the frightened man.

"What other man, I don't know..." Mike started to say.

"Drop the bull shit. We already got Raphael out of your building out back, and he told us there were two of you. You can call him in here now, or I can shoot you in the knee and then you can call him in here," Zach said, calmly as he put a comforting arm around Elise.

"Ok, ok, that's my girlfriend in the kitchen, Kitty. She's not feeling too good. And her brother Jerry, he's helping me keep an eye on everyone. I'll tell her to go get him, okay?" Mike asked, visibly trembling.

"Go ahead, but no funny stuff, or you lose a body part," Zach warned him, pointing the gun at his lower torso.

"Kitty, Kitty babe! Go find Jerry, we need him in here," Mike called down the stairwell, "there, nothing funny," He said to Zach.

They heard the back door open and close and a few minutes later it was opened again, followed by heavy, hurried footsteps. A young guy was about to run up the stairs when Zach stopped him.

"That's good, stay there, we're coming down." Zach motioned for Mad Mike to go down, then he and Elise followed. He directed everyone to sit at the big old country kitchen table, which they quickly did.

"All right, now that I have your attention, I want some information. No bull shit, I got plenty of that already. I get the right answers and no one gets hurt, and we are out of here in five minutes. Got it?" Zach asked of the three sitting in stunned silence in front of him. He got nods, but no one made a sound. "Mike, you first. Who hired you to grab Elise?"

Mike stared at Zach, then at the gun in his hand, then back at Zach. He cleared his throat a few times, then finally found his voice. "It was Harold Richardson. He paid me to grab her, and bring her here where no one would find her. He said no one was going to get hurt, he was giving her a better life!"

"Did it ever occur to you that she might not want that better life, or she would have went with him on her own?" Zach asked, leaning in a little closer to Mike. "Did he pay you to grab Raphael too?"

Mike sadly nodded and sank a little further into his chair.

"Did he pay you enough to make it worth your while to go to prison for twenty years, on kidnapping charges? Along with your two partners in crime here?"

Mike visibly paled, "no one said anything about jail time. He said he needed Elise brought here so he could offer her a better life! He just needed some time to talk to her," Mike blurted out, all gangster facade gone now, "and the guy we had in the shed, he just needed him someplace out of sight for a few days. I was supposed to keep him here for now, and Harold would let me know when to let him go. We weren't going to hurt him, his truck is sitting outside so he can just drive home in a few days!"

"Is Harold supposed to be coming out here? To talk to Elise? Or what's the plan?" Zach asked, needing to know if they could be expecting visitors any time soon. "You need to tell me everything you know. Harold is going to jail for a long, long time. If you don't want to go with him, you might want to consider talking to the DA and testifying against him."

"No, Harold told us to bring her here and lay low for a couple days, then he'd tell me what to do. He said don't hurt her, just keep her there and don't let her get away. He said his doctor friend, I met the guy once, Mathias I think, would be coming out to have a look at her, probably tonight." Mike was talking freely now.

Kitty and Jerry sat there through all of this, stone silent and unmoving. Zach figured they had little idea of what was actually going on. "What about you two? You getting paid by Harold too?" Zach turned his attention to the others.

"No, I don't know any Harold. Mikey asked me if he could bring a couple people here that he needed to hide for a while. I live here, I'm not doing anything wrong," Kitty explained without expression.

"Don't call me Mikey, I told you," Mad Mike quietly hissed at her, then turned to Zach. "Neither of them have anything to do with this whole thing. You gotta keep them out of it. Kitty's a good woman, just did what I asked her, with no questions. And Jerry is just a kid, he's not even twenty yet. I asked him to help me keep things under control. You know, walk around with me so it looks like there's more of us here," Mike explained lamely.

"What else can you tell me about what Harold is up to? What do you know about the apartment fire in Waukesha, a month ago, where a woman died? That was Elise's apartment, but it wasn't Elise, only made to look like it was her. How did that woman get there? Who set the fire? Was it you?" Zach hammered away at him.

"No! NO! That wasn't me! I didn't do any of that! That was…

uh, I'm not saying anything else," Mike said, realizing he already said too much. "I told you, all he wanted me to do was bring Elise here for a few days. Then the other guy too. That's it."

"That's not all and we both know it. You were seen leaving Harold's office a few days ago, with three other guys. The doctor, a guy named Eli, and one other guy. Who was that last guy?" Zach asked, "and what was that meeting about?"

"It was about getting Elise back, that's all! If you already know about the doctor and Eli, then you know Eli was the one who got Elise from her apartment. I don't know anything about the last guy, except he was pretty mean looking. Kind of scary," Mike insisted.

Zach stared coldly at Mike, who was visibly shaking now. "And you had no part in any of that? Are you sure?"

"Why don't you ask Eli this stuff? He knows what happened there."

"The police have him. He was already picked up a few days ago. Once he starts talking, he's the one to get the best deal from the DA you know," Zach said calmly. "And if he tells us you were a part of that apartment deal, you are going to be in some serious deep shit."

"I wasn't there….I….okay, look, all I did was help Eli bring a large heavy bag to the apartment," Mike said, his head in his hands, "then there was a woman there, kind of passed out. He said she was sick, so I helped him get her into his car. Then I left, and so did he, with the sick woman, which I learned later was Elise."

"What was in that heavy bag? What did it look like?" Zach asked, already knowing the answer.

"It was just a big long thing, kind of like a duffel bag, but pretty heavy. Needed two people to carry it. He said it was stuff she needed in her apartment. I didn't ask what was inside." Mike said sadly, then he raised his head and added, "but we didn't set the apartment on fire! We just left. There was no one else there, except the scary guy was standing on the corner. I saw him when I drove away."

"Then this scary guy, the fourth one at Harold's office must have started the fire, if you or Eli didn't. Don't you get it? That 'bag' you hauled in there was probably the woman who died in the fire." Zach stared intently at Mike, who looked like he had shrunk inside his pinstripe suit. "So what did this fourth guy look like?"

"Like I said, he was kind of scary looking. Mean. He had wild hair, kind of sticking up, all yellow and red. He was really dark skinned, Jamaican or something maybe. He didn't talk much, and I don't think anyone used his name. That's all I know, really!" Mike whined, "I thought Harold needed help finding her," he pointed at Elise who stood silently next to Zach though all of this.

"Did he say why he needed to find her?"

"Not exactly, just said it was worth a lot of money, millions upon millions and we'd all be handsomely rewarded if we brought her back to him." Mike said, unable to look at Elise anymore.

"You're about as pathetic as they come, you know that?" Zach said disdainfully as he narrowed his eyes at Mike. "Do you realize you're probably party to kidnapping, murder and arson, even if you didn't directly do all of it yourself? You're implicated. And now you're implicating your innocent girlfriend and her brother by bringing Elise and Raphael here. I don't think you grasp the trouble you're in. All for money. I hope it was a lot."

Zach pulled out his phone and called the police to come and pick up Mike and his accomplices. He was done talking to him and didn't think he'd get any more information from him anyway. When the police arrived, Zach explained a bit about the case and told them to call Scolari to figure out what to do with them. He took Elise to his truck, where Bastian and Raphael were anxiously waiting.

"You had us really scared when we saw the police coming," Bastian said, a huge look of relief on his face when he saw Elise come out of the farmhouse.

"We had a little talk, and now the police can have him. He didn't know a lot, but he did help move Elise out of her apartment and carry Liz into it. Whether she was dead or alive at that point I don't know," Zach said heavily. "Raphael, I think it's safe for you to go home, do you feel up to driving?"

"I sure do! My Marjorie will be so happy to see me! Thank you Mr. M! We have much to do, we need to find new jobs, I think Mr. R. won't be needing us too much longer," he gave a toothy grin as he jumped into his pickup and took off.

Zach turned to Elise. "You know, you could have gotten yourself killed doing something like this. If you want me to help you figure out this whole mess, fine. But if you keep throwing yourself into dangerous situations, I can't help you." He was more annoyed than he tried to sound, but this kind of thing had to stop. Now.

"I'm sorry, it's just that I feel so helpless, sitting around waiting for something to happen, or not happen. I want to get on with my life. My old life," Elise said quietly.

"I can totally understand that, but putting yourself in dangerous situations isn't helping you or the investigation. Let me do my job, and you just keep a low profile from here on out, all right?" Zach gave a deep annoyed sigh, trying to expel some of the annoyance he was feeling.

Chapter 19

After dropping Elise and Bastian off at their apartment building, with a stern warning to stay together at all times, Zach went back to his office. He needed some time to think. Kelly was just leaving for the day, but hung around to brainstorm with him a while.

"It sounds like it's all coming together, surely they can charge Harold with something now?" she asked.

"They picked him up, but haven't been able to hold him on anything. It's like his father said, he'd have an answer for everything they asked him." Zach grumbled, "I need to know who the fourth guy in the meeting was. He had to have set the fire, and possibly killed the woman. Maybe he'd roll on Harold. But how do I find out who he was? The only one who knows for sure is Harold, and he sure as hell isn't going to tell me." Suddenly Zach had a thought. "He might not, but someone close to him might."

"Who are you talking about?" Kelly asked, a puzzled look on her face.

"Harold's brother Edward said I should talk to their brother Thomas, since he wasn't quite as bad as Harold and the old man.

Might be worth a try. I'll give him a call in the morning," Zach sad, sounding hopeful once more.

"This is the most complicated case, honestly," Kelly said, shaking her head. "Who would ever believe someone would go to such lengths for money."

"A lot of people, I'm afraid," Zach said wearily. They locked up the office and called it a day.

The next morning, it took Zach several tries, but he finally managed to get through to set up a meeting with Thomas Richardson later that morning. Zach had no intention of a replay of his visit with Ernest, so this time the meeting was at a cafe down the street from the law office. Free until the meeting took place, he checked in with Bastian and Elise, to make sure nothing was happening there. Then he called his new friend at the Delafield Police station, Officer Patricia Lang, to see if anything was happening there. Luckily, she was available to talk to him.

"Things are moving along, but not in the direction you want to hear," she told Zach. "We didn't have enough to hold Harold or his father. Although he did sort of threaten you, there was no specific threat. And we can't charge him with condoning his son's bad behavior."

"Shit, I was afraid of that. What about that Dr. Mathias? Aren't there laws against practicing medicine with revoked license? And performing plastic surgery without a license?" Zach grumbled, "and what about the comatose woman in his basement? Melody?"

"First of all, we can't find the doctor, his housekeeper said he is on an extended vacation. She let a few of our guys go through the house, but there was no sign of a woman in any condition in the basement or anywhere else. They said the basement looks like a storage area, not set up as a hospital room. So if she was there, she isn't now. We could charge him with writing prescriptions without a valid license, but that's about it," Officer Lang explained to Zach.

"I don't believe it. He's going to get away with it?" Zach couldn't believe his ears. "What if a couple of his partners in crime would testify against him?"

"That would change everything, but so far no one is doing that. Eli, the young guy who was picked up after trying to grab Elise in the park isn't rolling over on Harold. He claims he was mugging Elise and didn't know she was the one he delivered the pizza to. Claims not to even know Harold," she told him.

"Another of his paid thugs is in custody, as of yesterday, guy by the name of Mike Walker. He did admit to me that him and Eli dropped a large package off in Elise's apartment, the night of the fire, and that he helped Eli take Elise to his car. He said Eli told him she was sick. He also said Harold paid them to get Elise back," Zach started to explain all that had transpired at the farmhouse the day before.

"Hold it, the Racine police brought him to us last night, as part of an ongoing investigation. He was questioned at length, and his story now seems to vary quite a bit from what he told you. He said you threatened to shoot him and his girlfriend, so he was scared and said whatever you wanted him to say. So his story to you is out the window." Patricia Lang wasn't thrilled to be the bearer of such lousy news, but there was no good way to explain it. "And of course, he isn't rolling on Harold either."

They were both promised a lot of money to keep their mouths shut and deliver Elise to him." Zach said, "hey, what about grabbing Raphael? We found him at that farmhouse too, tied up in an outbuilding."

"This Mike guy did admit to that, but didn't say he did it for

Harold. Said he was just horsing around with the guy, he got mad, so Mike tied him up to let him cool off, and was going to let him go, then you showed up. We can't get Raphael to file a complaint against him, either."

"So there has to be some way to get one or more of these guys to turn on Harold. Once that happens, the whole thing will collapse on top of him. I have to find that weak link. There has to be one," Zach said, determination clear in his voice. He thanked Officer Lang for her time, and took off for his meeting with yet another of the Richardson clan.

Thomas Richardson was already comfortably seated in the cafe when Zach arrived. They exchanged pleasant greetings and he sat down. Zach laid out a condensed version of everything that was going on, taking his time to see if he could read Thomas at all. But Thomas was hard to read. He listened carefully, never interrupted and barely changed his facial expression at all. When Zach finally finished, Thomas played with his coffee spoon for a moment, then quietly spoke.

"Sounds like quite a mess my brother has gotten himself into. Not too incredibly surprising, as he will do anything to acquire more of the all-mighty dollar. But this whole scheme is beyond even him." Thomas shook his head, looking annoyed, and asked, "so what is it you want from me? Since I knew nothing of this elaborate plot, I can't affirm or deny any of it happened as you say it has."

"I talked to your younger brother Edward not long ago, and he's the one who suggested I talk to you. Just a long shot I'm afraid, but I was hoping there was anything you could tell me that would validate any part of this whole story," Zach said, knowing he didn't have anything specific to ask him for.

"Well, I can say that myself and my wife, along with my sister and her family, all met this woman he was passing off as his wife. He introduced her as Melody, and explained she had some sort of amnesia from the accident. Since I didn't know at the time it wasn't Melody, I had no reason to think it wasn't. She looked a little different, but she also had bruising and bandages on her face. She looked a little younger, which I attributed to a week's rest, and she didn't have the usual hardness to her look. I'm only saying this in retrospect, like I said, I wasn't focused on her that evening. She talked very little, we had dinner, and that was about it. So if there was some crime committed having her there in Melody's place, so be it," Thomas said, as he tried to remember anything more from that evening.

"Nothing that could be used in court I'm afraid," Zach said, disappointed.

"Other than that, I'm afraid there's not much else I can tell you. We all thought it was rather odd, when a few days after that dinner, Harold told us she took a turn for the worse and was rehospitalized. She didn't seem like she was critically injured. A few facial injuries, a foot in a cast and amnesia. Nothing life threatening to require another extended stay in a hospital, with no visitors, no phone calls, nothing. We chalked it up to Harold and his extreme eccentric ways," Thomas said as he rose to leave. "Now, if that's all, I do need to get to work."

"Thank you, I do appreciate you meeting with me, even if you didn't help me find the smoking gun. It has to be somewhere." Zach rose and shook the man's hand.

"In truth, I hope you do figure it out. Harold needs to learn that there are limits, that even he has to abide by. If he's really responsible for killing a woman, kidnapping another, and all the other mayhem you spoke of, he should be held accountable. If that works in my favor in our father's eyes, that's all right too," he said with a chuckle. "Harold can be reckless, and I've always told him that one day his actions will come back to bite him in the ass. He takes on clients that no one else in the firm will touch, because he likes the thrill of it. Sometimes people that belong behind bars, but yet he takes them on as clients and frequently gets them off. I saw one of those characters leaving his office just the other day. A known arsonist that goes by the name Flame. The guy is bad news, and yet, here he is, coming out of Harold's office like he doesn't have a care in the world." Thomas shook his head.

"Wait! An arsonist named Flame?" Zach's heart rate jumped. "Does he happen to be a Jamaican, with red and yellow hair?"

"Haha, you've met him? That's Flame all right, why do you ask?" Thomas said, stopping in his tracks.

"Do you happen to know what his real name is or where I can find him?" Zach asked, holding his breath.

"That's an easy one, come on, take a walk with me to my office," Thomas offered, then added, "so, you think he might be the one who started the fire in that apartment?"

"I do. I'm almost positive," Zach said, the adrenaline pumping in his veins.

In his office, Thomas offered Zach a seat while he went through the files on his computer. It didn't take long before he had exactly the information Zach had been praying for.

"Okay, here we are. Flame, real name Delroy Jones, from Cudahy, no less. Suspected of numerous arson fires, but only ever served time twice. He walked on all the other charges for one reason or another. My brother represented him in a few of those cases, let me see here," Thomas scrolled down pages of legal jargon, looking for something that Zach could use. "Here we are, I thought there was something going on the last time he was charged. They claimed extenuating circumstances at his home, so for him to serve jail time, it would cause undue hardship on the family."

"So he didn't go to jail?" Zach was puzzled by this.

"Well, it was a weak case anyway, the witness wasn't the greatest, and Flame had a good lawyer, namely Harold. So I'm guessing he feels like he owes Harold," Thomas said as he continued to scroll. "He has a child at home with Cerebral Palsy. Needs a lot of care, so him and his wife take turns tending to his needs. The last arson case was weak, and putting Flame in jail would ultimately punish the child, so Harold was able to get the charges dropped. He does treatments on the child several times a day, and he's on a list for a lung transplant. Flame feels responsible for the kids condition, since it's inherited. Anyway, might be useful information if you need it." Thomas wrote an address on a piece of paper and gave it to Zach.

"I can't tell you how much I appreciate this. He's the last missing part of the puzzle, and if I can convince him to talk, everything else will fall in place," Zach said, shaking Thomas' hand heartily.

"Good luck, I'm not sure how it'll go with him, but I do think it's time Harold paid for his bad behavior," Thomas said as he walked Zach out of the building. "But just for the record, you got none of this information from me."

Zach wasted no time at all driving straight to Cudahy, a town just outside of Milwaukee on the south east side. He found the address and bounded up the stairs of the porch. Before he had a chance to knock, a small boy answered the door.

"My folks ain't home," he said flatly.

"Do you know when they will be home? I need to talk to your

dad," Zach said to the solemn child.

"My mom went to get my medicine, she'll be back in a couple minutes. I wanted to go with her, but she said, not today," the little boy wheezed as he spoke softly.

Zach's heart went out to the little boy, who looked to be close in age to his own son Nathan, who had just turned eight. He wondered if this little guy had ever had a chance to ride a bike or play catch with his father. Still, he needed to talk to Flame, and if Flame cooperated, maybe Zach could see about getting him some help for his son. He looked like he could use it.

"When do you think your dad is coming home?" Zach asked the child.

"He was supposed to already be home, that's why my mom went to get my medicine, cuz my dad was supposed to be here with me," the boy said, "they don't like me staying by myself, in case I can't breath. I have CF."

"How about I sit here on the porch with you, until your mom or dad comes home? Would that be okay?" Zach asked.

"Yeah, I guess so, you can't come inside, and I'm not going nowhere with you, but you can sit on the porch, sure." The boy seemed to be trying to determine if this was within the rules his parents had set for him, and decided it must be all right.

"Do you have any brothers or sisters?" Zach asked the boy, mostly to pass time.

"No, my mom said they might have CF too, so they didn't think it was a good idea. They said when I get better, I might get a puppy though," the child said, his dark little face showing some animation for the first time.

"I have a puppy, though he's not too little anymore," Zach told the boy, "it's a German Shepherd and his name is Rudy."

"Awww, that's neat," the boy said with a wide toothed smile.

"Cordell! What are you doing? Get in the house, boy," came a stern voice from the sidewalk, as Flame walked up to the porch. The boy hopped up and scooted inside.

"Who the hell are you, and what are you doing on my porch, with my boy?" Flame nearly spat as he approached Zach.

"The name's Zach. I'm here looking for you. I think we can be of great service to each other," Zach said with a smile as he offered his hand to the muscular man with the wild red and yellow hair.

"I doubt that," Flame said as he crossed his arms in front of his broad chest and took a couple steps closer to Zach.

Chapter 20

"Maybe not, but at least hear me out," Zach said, unmoving, and unimpressed with Flame's threatening stance.

"You got five minutes," Flame said.

"I know who you are, and what you do, and to some extent, who you do it for." Zach spoke, not too sure where to start. "I'm not really concerned with all of that. What I am concerned with is a job you did for Harold Richardson last month, an apartment fire."

"Don't know what you're talking abou," Flame said slowly. Zach could see the muscles twitching in his jaw, and the slight narrowing of his eyes.

"Let me be quick and blunt. I need you to testify against Harold in court, and implicate Eli and Mad Mike in the apartment fire, leaving the woman in there to burn in place of Elise Taggert, and the kidnapping of Elise," Zach stated and waited for a response.

"That's a pretty tall order. Not that I'm saying I know anything about any of this, but if I did, why would I be so stupid to testify and implicate myself along with the others?" Flame said with a smirk.

"A few reasons. One, you can turn state's evidence for immunity on your part, and you'd be able to stay out of jail and watch your son grow up. Two, Harold is going down with or without your help, and either way, you are implicated. So if the police get someone else to turn on Harold, you go down with him. And then who's going to be around to help raise your son?" Zach told him bluntly, "and three, if you do this, I can get you some assistance you need for your son."

"I don't need help for my boy, I take good care of him. His mother and I do," Flame said defiantly, but his tone had softened somewhat. "We are doing everything we can for him, until he can get a lung transplant. What are you going to do, give him one of yours?"

"No, but did you know there are new meds coming out all the time to treat CF? And programs to give you and his mom help in caring for him? Like someone to come in a couple times a week so the two of you could go out, together even, once in a while. There's even week long summer camps he could go to, where every kid there has CF and all the camp counselors and staff know how to treat the kids. He'd love it, he'd meet kids like him, and you and his mom would get a little break. What about things like that?" Zach listed a few programs that were available to anyone that took the time to research them. He had a hunch Flame and his wife didn't. "With some of the improvements they've made in the treatments, he might even be able to go to school."

"I wasn't aware of some of that," Flame said softly, "but we can't afford a lot of those extras for him. We do the best we can."

"They won't cost you anything. I would have my office manager help you apply for every single program you're eligible for. It could be a life changer for your son," Zach said, motioning to the boy who was standing just inside the doorway, listening to the conversation. "Now that he's old enough to know what's going on around him, you might want to consider turning your life around and becoming a good example for him."

"Who the hell are you to come strolling up to my porch to tell me how to raise my son and how to live my life? And on top of all that, you need me to rat on Harold? Know what happens to snitches in the slammer?"

"You wouldn't have to be in jail. And like it or not, you're the main influence in your son's life. Do you want him to grow up to be a criminal? Don't you want more for him than that?" Zach asked, knowing he was pushing his luck. "You seem like a pretty smart guy, I don't think you'd have too much trouble finding honest work."

Flame stood silent for a minute, a stoney cold glare on his face. Then surprisingly, his voice softened a little as he finally spoke again. "Yeah, my uncle's got a garage a few miles from here. Always asking me to come and learn the ropes and work with him. Never did cuz I like to be able to keep an eye on things here," Flame said with a weary sigh. "I wouldn't mind learning a trade for an honest wage. Would probably feel pretty good, you know?"

"That sounds like a real good idea. I have a son about the same age as your boy, and he is fascinated with my work. Wants to be just like me when he grows up," Zach laughed. "His mom has other plans for him, but for now, he wants to be just like his dad. Your son is probably no different."

"All right mister do-gooder, you caught me at a weak moment," Flame almost laughed, and Zach could sense the relief in his voice. "I will help you take Harold down. Guy's a jerk anyway. But for the record, I did not kill that woman. He had a dead body in a bag delivered to that apartment. I start fires. I don't kill people."

"Fair enough. I'd like you to come with me to see a detective friend of mine, and we can get your whole story taken down. Then we can finally put Harold behind bars where he belongs," Zach offered.

"Yeah, let's get this whole thing done with, before I have a change of heart," Flame agreed. He made sure his wife had returned home to be with their son, and he left willingly with Zach.

Zach was surprised by how readily Flame had agreed to come with him and expose Harold, but he was glad he did, for whatever reason. Harold seemed to have an endless list of people who didn't care much for him.

They drove to Scolari's office, but on the way, Zach called Officer Lang in the Delafield police department, in case she wanted to join them there, which she did. Scolari was waiting for them when they all arrived at about the same time. He ushered them into a large interrogation room and set the recorder on the table. He stated a few facts about what was going on, and told Flame to start talking. And he did.

Flame told them how he had been contacted by Harold, and had asked him to come to his office for a meeting one day. He reminded Flame how he had kept him out of jail. Once at the office, he was introduced to Eli and Mad Mike, and told he'd be doing a job with the two of them. Harold told him he needed an apartment torched, so it looked like an electrical fire. Harold said he knew Flame was looking to get out of that line of work, but this last job would pay $50,000. Everyone listened carefully as Flame sat and talked in his deep voice with the lilting Jamaican accent.

"When I asked him why he was willing to pay so much for an apartment fire, Harold told me there needed to be a body burned in the fire. Burned badly enough to make identifying it difficult. I told him I don't kill people in my fires, no matter what the price was, and he told me not to worry, he was personally making sure the body was very dead. And it was. There was a young woman in a duffle bag in the apartment when I got there. I watched from the street when Eli and Mad Mike hauled the bag into the building, and left a few minutes later with an unconscious woman. As soon as they drove away, I went to the apartment, took the body out of the bag, laid her out to look like she was sleeping on the sofa, worked my magic in the place and left."

"Did you check the woman at all to make sure she was dead?" Scolari asked.

"I did, but it was pretty obvious. She was cold and gray. Had to have been dead a few hours already. And she still had a plastic bag on her head." Flame stated. "I tossed the plastic bag, but I took the duffle bag home with me. It's all cloth, so I don't think you'll get any prints off it."

"All right, we'll want to get that bag from you later," Scolari said, "go on."

"Well, after the fire, I got one call from Harold, saying it was a perfect job and I'd be getting paid for it very soon. Then I didn't hear from him for a few weeks I guess, and I got a call to get my ass to his office the following morning. I figured he was going to pay me, so I went. When I got there, Eli and Mad Mike were there too, and some other guy he referred to as the doctor, or Ray. I gotta tell you, Harold was out of control that morning. I thought the guy was going to have a stroke or something. He kept yelling and ranting at everyone in the room, about how he had to have that woman grabbed again. Said he'd make it worth our while and we had to get her to him, like yesterday. I don't know why he had me in that meeting, I start fires, you know? I don't nab people. Anyway, the others assured him they'd get her, no problem. He said if we didn't mess this up, we'd all be millionaires," Flame said with a nervous laugh. "I left his office and haven't seen or heard from him since, including not getting my money for my work in the apartment. I don't know if the others grabbed the woman for him again or not."

"So he hasn't actually paid you yet? No money exchanged hands?" Scolari said, his teeth clenched.

"No, but the others in the office at either meeting, they all heard the same things I did. They'll back me up, I'm sure." Flame said.

"Well so far, no one is admitting to anything. You're the first who has actually implicated Harold, and all we have is your word. No proof. No way to prove he told you to set that fire." Scolari said with a sigh.

"Well, what do you expect? He didn't write it down or anything," Flame shrugged casually. He didn't appear ruffled that it was his word against Harold's. "I however, did the next best thing."

"What do you mean?" Zach had to ask.

"I taped the conversations, both of them. Just hit the record button on my phone in my pocket. These new smart phones are so damn handy sometimes. I know they can't be used in court, but you might find them handy for convincing the others to back me up," Flame said with a slight smile. "But I would like to know for sure that I am not going to be charged with anything. I get immunity, right?"

"If you actually have taped conversations with Harold and the others, and we can verify it's him on the tape, you have a deal. But we need to hear them," Scolari said, rising up in his chair.

"I made a point of calling him by name more than once," Flame said with a grin as he pulled his cell phone from his pocket. He hit the recorder application and slid the phone across the table to Scolari.

Everyone listened to the recorded conversation for a few minutes. The voice giving the orders was definitely Harold. And true to his word, Flame did call Harold by name more than once. After a few minutes of the recording, Scolari was convinced.

"Sounds good to me, you have yourself a deal, Flame," he nodded.

"Sounds good enough for me to call and have Harold picked up," Officer Lang said, reaching for her phone. She made a quick call, then we all listened to the rest of the recordings.

As the recording finished, Zach's phone sounded in his pocket, about the same time Officer Lang's phone was ringing. They both took their calls. Zach could see the disappointed and annoyed look on her face as she spoke into her phone, at the same time he was answering his. It was Bastian.

"Zach, I hate to say this, but she's gone," he said, fear making his voice crack.

Chapter 21

"How? When?!" Zach asked, alarmed.

"She was in her apartment, locked in nice and safe, not going anywhere. I was home. She said she'd call if she was going anywhere," Bastian said, sounding a little out of breath. "I heard a commotion in the hall and looked out, but by the time I was out there, the elevator doors were closing. I had a bad feeling, so I ran over to her apartment. The door was closed, but unlocked, and she was gone. It looks like there was a bit of a scuffle in there."

"So you have no idea who took her? When did this happen?" Zach barked into the phone, throwing helpless looks to everyone in the room.

"Just now, a couple minutes ago! I ran down the stairs hoping to beat the elevator, but by the time I got down, all I saw was a car pulling away from the curb, in a big hurry. There wasn't anyone else in the building lobby, and the elevator was open and empty." Bastian said, "So I called you right away."

"Did you get a look at the car? License number possibly?" Zach asked, the wheels turning in his brain as he spoke.

"There was no plate on the back of the car. It was black, a Lexus

I think, or maybe a Lincoln. One of those expensive SUVs. I'm so sorry, Zach," Bastian said, feeling he was to blame.

"It wasn't your fault, she was in her apartment. I wonder who she opened the door for?" Zach muttered. "I gotta go, I'll catch you later."

"Elise is gone, again. Someone grabbed her right out of her apartment," Zach said to the others in the room. "Dammit, who did it now? Don't you have everyone in custody?"

"Not everyone. That was my precinct calling. Harold can't be found," Officer Lang said.

"That means he grabbed her himself! He's getting desperate.," Zach said, color rising to his face. "Where would he take her now?"

"I wish we had any idea. Not to his house, not to Dr. Mathias' place, and we know of no other home he has," Scolari said. "Flame? Any ideas?"

Flame shook his head reluctantly. He had nothing.

"Wait! I wonder if she took her cell phone with her! I have to call Bastian back," Zach said as he punched in the number. "Bastian, is her phone in her apartment? Go look, fast! Wait, better yet, turn on that app you both put on your phones, so you could track her - is it working, is she moving?"

Bastian fumbled with his phone for a second, then came back with the answer Zach was dying to hear. "Yeah, it's working! She's on the move! Looks like they're heading east on highway 18."

"Keep watching it, we're going to chase him down!" Zach said as he jumped up and motioned for anyone to follow him. "He's tracking her movements on her phone, with some app they both installed!" Zach explained as he tore out of the room. Officer Lang followed him immediately. After a second's hesitation, Scolari got up as well. "Hang tight, we need to wrap this up when we get back," he said to Flame as he followed Zack and Lang out of the building.

The three of them jumped into Lang's squad car, and with lights flashing and sirens wailing, they tore down the road. Zach barked out directions from the back seat as quickly as Bastian gave them to him. From highway 18, Harold and his passenger made their way onto interstate 45, then 41, heading north out of the city. The squad car had come from the east side of Milwaukee, while Harold was coming from the west. It wasn't long before they were only a few miles behind him. They turned off their lights and sirens and stayed back far enough that he wouldn't spot them, and relied on Bastian's reports of his movements.

He exited on highway 60, going west, through the small towns of Slinger and Hartford, and kept going. "Where the hell is he taking her?" Zach muttered to no one in particular.

"Okay, looks like he's getting somewhere now, turning left, uh, south I guess, on Jefferson road. Looks pretty bare out there, wherever they are," Bastian reported. His heart was racing as he relayed the info as soon as he got it. He knew Elise's life could depend on it. "Another turn, right on Pond Road. He appears to be slowing down, the road might be gravel or dirt, can't really tell."

"You're doing great Bastian, we're right behind him, just out of sight." Zach said. "What's he doing now?"

"Okay, they went off the end of the road as far as it shows on the map. Still going straight from there. I'm looking at a satellite view of the area, it looks like nothing there but trees," Bastian said, growing anxious.

"I have the same area on my phone map, on Google Maps, so I can see exactly what you're telling me, this is good," Zach encouraged him, knowing how scared he must be for Elise.

"They're going really slow now, hardly moving. Maybe they're walking," Bastian said as panic raised his voice a few octaves, "wait, it looks like there's a small body of water up ahead. Hurry Zach, you better get to her fast!"

"We're right there, we see his car," Zach told Bastian, "now we're walking down a path, we can see a lake ahead of us, they have to be right ahead of us. I'm going to stop talking now, but I'm still here," he whispered.

"She stopped. She's not moving anymore," Bastian said, holding his breath, "her dot is just sort of bouncing around a little in the same spot."

Officer Lang and Scolari took the lead as they moved as quickly as they could down the rocky path leading to the little lake. Scolari motioned for Zach to stay by the car, but Zach being who he was, ignored Scolari and followed. Zach reasoned he was getting the instructions from Bastian, so needed to go, and he was doing no one any good standing by the empty squad car. So he followed close on the heels of the two officers. As they turned to follow a bend in the path, the lake came fully into view on their right. There was a very small, worn cabin sitting right along the shoreline, next to an equally forlorn looking pier.

Scolari stopped, motioning for everyone behind him to stop as well.

"Zach, this is as far as you can go. He might be armed." Scolari drew his revolver and nodded for Lang to follow him. She too drew her weapon and the two of them made their way down the final hundred feet of the path, to the edge of the pier.

Zach stood, teeth clenched, on the path where Scolari had told him to wait. This was doing no one any good, he thought to himself.

Zach stood motionless for a few seconds, the muscles in his

jaw twitching as he decided what to do. Silently, he left the path, creeping through the tall brush, until he came out on the rocky shore on the opposite side of the house. He crept silently to the corner of the house, and stopped, straining to hear what was going on inside. Zach took a few steps further, to a small dirty window. He didn't risk looking in, since he'd be too visible if anyone looked out, but the temptation was great.

On the pier, Scolari and Lang cautiously approached the cabin, the old pier creaking with every step they took. There was no way their arrival was going to be a surprise. Scolari reached the door, ready to open it, and Lang was ready, her gun aimed at whatever was behind it.

"Police! Harold, we're coming in!" Scolari yelled as he burst into the cabin, Lang on his heels.

Harold stood in the middle of the room, facing them. He had one arm tightly around Elise, and in his other hand, a gun to her temple. "Welcome to the party, officers, come in," he said with a sneer, "the fun's just beginning."

"Harold, we have the place surrounded. It's all over," Scolari said calmly. "Put the gun down, and let her go."

"The thing is, officer, I know it's all over. So I have nothing to lose anymore, do I? If I shoot her, you shoot me, and it's all over with. Or I drop my gun, and you arrest me and I go to jail." Harold stared coldly at Scolari. "I'm not sure that's any better than being shot, do you think? Can't you people see that she's ruined everything? You all have! Why did you have to meddle?"

"We weren't meddling, Harold. You killed a woman and kidnapped another. That's not meddling. Those are called crimes," Scolari stated, his gun still trained on Harold's chest.

"All I wanted to do was give a struggling woman, living a

miserable pauper's life, a majestic new life! Is that so wrong?" Harold spat the words out, spraying his spittle on the side of Elise's face.

"You can't really believe that. If you wanted to offer her this grand opportunity, how about do it over a cup of coffee? Not by staging an accident, drugging her in hopes that she'd lose her memory, getting your real wife out of the way, and killing another innocent woman." Lang spoke up in her soft, but firm voice.

"Damn all of you," Harold hissed as he took a few steps backward, pulling Elise along with him. "Stay back, all of you, or she dies. I've got nothing to lose by killing her, I'm already going to jail for murder, remember?"

Harold inched his way toward the back door, where the little cabin hung out over the lake. Scolari and Lang stood their ground, not making any move toward Harold.

Zach could hear the bits of the heated exchange through the tired old walls. Silently, he inched his way around to the back corner of the cabin. Peeking around the corner, he could see the door that Harold was working his way closer to. There was a narrow pier running along the back of the cabin, less than three feet wide. As luck would have it, there was a large rain barrel on the corner, large enough for Zach to crouch behind. Which he did. And waited for the back door to open. Which it did, before very long.

Zach heard the jiggling of the doorknob before he saw the door slowly start to open. He wasn't entirely sure who was coming through it, but he had hopes it was going to be Harold. But it was Elise who opened the door, not Harold. For an instant, Zach was baffled, then he saw Harold's hand firmly gripping her arm, and a gun aimed at her head. What the hell was he planning to do now? Zach waited a moment, expecting to see Scolari or Lang coming through the door behind them, but nothing. The rickety door closed with a slam. Watching thru a narrow gap between the corner of the cabin and the rain barrel, Zach could see Harold talking quietly to Elise, his mouth close to her ear. The gun in his hand was dangerously close to her head, but then he began to wave it around. First at the side of her head, then at the side of his, then back at her. Zach sucked in his breath and waited, poised and ready to react. Harold began to wave the gun again, and Zach took aim and quickly squeezed off a shot, winging Harold in the upper arm.

"Ahhhhh! AaaahhHHHHH!!" Harold howled like a wounded animal as he grabbed the arm that had been shot, releasing his grip on Elise. "You shot me! I'm hit!"

With a hopeless, panicked look on his face, Harold grabbed Elise again, and in the same swift movement, raised the gun with his injured arm.

"Harold! No!!" Zach yelled as he burst out from behind the rain barrel. A shot rang out, so close, it stunned Zach for an instant.

"Noooo!" Scolari yelled as he and Lang burst through the back door. In the same second, Harold fell backward into the lake, taking Elise with him. Zach dropped his jacket and instantly jumped into the icy cold lake. He dove under the water, searching frantically for the two. He came up, gasping for a few seconds and went down again. Finally he spotted them and swam faster than he thought possible. The water was cloudy red, but he managed to grab Elise's arm and pull her to the surface. Scolari had jumped into the water too, and was there to help her get to the pier. Zach dove down again, but didn't see Harold anywhere. He came up again, out of breath.

"What the hell just happened?" Scolari yelled, to no one in particular. "Zach, I thought I told you to stay on the hill?"

"I don't do well with standing on hills," Zach said as he swam back to the pier. "Where did he go now?" he asked of Harold as he nodded to the lake.

They all turned to look at the lake, at about the spot Harold had fallen in. There was no sign of him.

"I only shot him in the arm, he isn't mortally wounded," Zach said quietly, a feeling of unease coming over him. Where had the man gone so quickly?

They both climbed back onto the pier where Lang was looking over Elise. Zach picked up his his jacket from where he had tossed it on the pier, and wrapped it around her shivering body.

"Are you okay?" Zach gasped, trying to catch his breath. "Did he shoot you?"

"No…..I'm fine." Elise said, looking about as un-fine as a person could. "He shot himself, in the head I think, and grabbed my arm as he fell backward."

"Where is he, if he shot himself in the head?" Zach said, spinning around, looking in all directions, the same as Scolari and Lang were doing.

It was eerily silent as the four of them stood there, scanning the lake in all directions. The water was still, as if it had already forgotten about the turmoil that had just taken place under its surface.

Scolari held up a finger to his lips, then pointed straight down, under the pier. Everyone froze. Everyone but Zach, who turned and jumped sideways into the water, and under the pier. Sure enough, there was Harold, blood still streaming from somewhere on his head, fumbling with the pistol in his hand, as if trying to shoot from under the pier. Zach came up next to him so quickly, he didn't have time to react.

"Shit Zach, are you trying to get yourself killed?" Scolari grumbled as he leaned down and tried to see what was going on under the pier. Happily, Zach reappeared almost instantly, dragging a weakly struggling Harold under his chin. Scolari and Lang quickly pulled Harold onto the pier, then helped Zach up as well.

On the pier, they could see that Harold had sort of shot himself in the head, with the bullet taking off the top of his ear and then skimming up and off the top of his head. If he was trying to kill himself, it was a really lousy attempt. Harold was quickly hand-cuffed, and escorted, kicking and groaning, off the pier, through the cabin and up the path. Shivering and cold, with only Lang still in dry clothes, they all made their way back to the cars, where Lang pulled several blankets from the trunks and helped everyone wrap themselves in them. She grabbed several gauze pads from the first aid kit and crudely taped them to the side of Harold's head, and around his upper arm. Shivering, they all piled into the car and left. Harold's adventure was finally over.

"Zach? Zach? What the hell is going on?" Bastian's panicky voice was heard from Zach's jacket pocket, where he had left his phone. With a weary smile, Zach handed his phone to Elise, happy she had good news to give him at last.

Chapter 22

The next few weeks were a blurry haze of activities for everyone involved. Harold's minor injuries were tended to and he was escorted off to jail. He immediately demanded his phone call, to his own office, to procure a lawyer. Not too surprisingly, both his father and brother Thomas declined the offer, and his case was turned over to someone else in the firm. The testimonies and evidence against Harold were strong enough that he was denied bail, much to everyone's relief. Harold would be looking at four gray walls for a long, long time.

Before too long, everyone was getting their lives back to normal. Marjorie, Raphael and Marie were able to quickly find new work, since so many of Harold's friends and acquaintences knew of them and their reliability. They had several offers and were happy to accept one from an older couple who took all three of them together. Their new living quarters and salaries were a nice step up from what they had at the Richardson home, which made the move even easier.

Officer Lang had been able to tell Zach that Raymond Mathias was picked up in Iowa, trying to sell his home from there. He had been brought back to Wisconsin and had a number of charges pending against him, including murder or accessory to murder in the case of the real Melody Richardson. In exchange for leniency, he confessed to the drugging of both women, and to helping Harold dispose of Melody's body once she had died as a result of all the drugs she'd been given. They had buried her in a shallow grave up near Harold's old cottage on Green Lake. Mathias also admitted to giving Harold a lethal drug to administer to Liz before leaving her in the apartment that went up in flames. He had provided the drugs to knock out Elise when she was taken from her apartment. He denied doing any of Elise's plastic surgery and refused to say any more on that subject, but it wasn't of much importance so they weren't pushing him on that issue.

Elise was back in her apartment, all brand new yet still old and comfortable. She was busier than ever with her dog training, and was planning to add a dog of her own to her life very soon. She was happy the nightmare was all over and behind her and she could move on with her life. But other times, when she thought about all that had happened, she wondered if she could have somehow prevented it. What if she hadn't accepted the cup of coffee from Harold that day he bumped into her. Maybe none of this would have happened, and Melody and Liz would still be alive. Bastian and Zach had both reassured her repeatedly that none of what happened was her doing. It was all on Harold's head. She knew she was going to have to testify at his trial, and at first the thought had terrified her. But as time went by, and she had more time to think about all the people he had hurt, her fear turned to anger and she was now anxious to help put him behind bars.

As for Bastian, he was still working as a clown, but he had

caught the bug for investigative work and popped in on Zach a couple times a week. Zach thoroughly enjoyed the unconventional Bastian, and the two quickly became good friends.

Zach was preparing to move into his new home, right above his office. When he told his son Nathan about the move, and about him having his own bedroom there, the young boy was excited beyond belief. The first thing he asked was if Rudy could sleep in there with him on the nights Nathan was there. Zach of course thought that was a great idea.

In the middle of all his packing, Zach came across the box that his outdoor motion sensor camera had come in. It was empty. Zach puzzled over this for a few minutes, then suddenly recalled hiding it in the bushes by the law firm, and never remembering to remove it. He made a mental note to go look for it the following day on his way to work. After sitting there for several weeks, the SD card had to be full by now, and the batteries maybe even dead, but it was still a useful piece of equipment.

After picking up the camera in the morning, that was surprisingly undisturbed, and still running, Zach headed for his office. He was getting excited about his upcoming move. Living right above his own office was about as cool as it could get, he thought with a silly grin. He stuck the SD card in his computer and watched as literally hundreds and hundreds of low res images popped up. He wasn't sure what he was looking for anymore, since Harold was already behind bars, but he scrolled through the images anyway. It was good to learn how useful the camera could be, if nothing else. Over half the images were birds or leaves that got right in front of the lens, and even a few snouts from some inquisitive dogs. Other than that, just a lot of people going in and out of the law firm. He recognized Ernest and Harold several times, as well as Thomas, but no one else. He was getting close to the end of the photos when his phone rang. Only half paying attention to the repetitive images, he picked up the phone. It was Elise, who wanted to meet him for lunch. Zach accepted, wondering what was on her mind. Then, just as he hung up, he spotted an interesting image. It was Elise going into the firm's front doors! Was that possible? Why would she be going there? He checked the date and time stamp on that image and saw it was taken only two days ago. What was going on there? He would be sure and ask her over lunch, which she had conveniently just arranged.

At the restaurant, Elise looked much better than the last time Zach had seen her. All her bruising had completely disappeared and her tiny scars were invisible. She was a very attractive woman, he thought. They had an enjoyable lunch, chatting about their busy lives and the insanity of people like Harold. Zach patiently waited to see if she would bring up anything about visiting the law firm office.

"I still have a hard time believing someone would go to that much trouble, all for money. To do all that he did with the hopes of latching onto his father's fortune, and have no regard for all the lives he hurt, is almost impossible to fathom," Elise said as they had coffee after their meal.

"Unfortunately, people do horrible things for a lot less money than what Harold was after," Zach told her, sadly shaking his head.

"I suppose you're wondering why I asked you to lunch," Elise said, color coming into her cheeks as she spoke. "I went to see Thomas, Harold's brother, the other day, and had a long interesting chat with him. I was very happy to learn he didn't share his brother's ethics."

"You went to see Thomas? Why?" Zach asked. He wasn't sure

why she wanted to meet him for lunch, but to tell him she had met with Thomas wasn't even on his list of possibilities.

"I went to see him, to get this," she said as she pushed an envelope across the table to Zach.

With a baffled frown on his face, Zach took the envelope and opened it. Inside was a very substantial check written out to him, from Thomas! Zach could find no words for a second or two.

"It occurred to me a while ago that while you were running all over the place figuring things out, you weren't billing anyone for anything! I mean, it should have been me, but you never billed me or brought up the money or discussed it whenever I brought it up. I got to thinking about that, and decided it was Harold who should pay your bill, since this was all his doing," Elise explained, "so I went to his brother and told him that. And he agreed!"

"This was very nice of you to do, but the amount is way too much. I can't accept this," Zach said.

"Oh yes you can. It's a done deal. Thomas decided on the amount, not me, and he really wanted you to have it. He said a lot of people would have given up on such a complicated case. He said he'd like to know he could call you if he was ever in a jam," Elise told him firmly.

"I really appreciate you doing that. This is a pretty incredible sum, what did he base it on, how they bill their hours?" Zach said with a low whistle.

"I don't know, and I didn't ask. I just gave him the facts, and suggested he come up with an appropriate figure. I know you'll never get rich in your line of work, but what you do for people is pretty priceless. I have you to thank for having my life back. Who can put a price tag on that?" Elise said, still flushed with color.

They drank the rest of their coffee and and parted ways, after

Elise gave Zach one last big giant hug. "Saying thank you seems so inadequate, but I do thank you so much. I'm so happy to have my whole life back. All the simple things I took for granted, I enjoy them even more than before. I can go for a walk whenever and wherever I want without looking over my shoulder," she told him sincerely. "And if you ever need any help training your dog, you know who to call."

"I will certainly do that, probably sooner rather than later, before Rudy picks up too many bad habits," Zach told her, returning her hug. "And thank you again for this." Zach said as he lightly slapped the envelope in the palm of his hand a few times.

Zach drove back to the office with a smile on his face. Another case closed with a positive outcome. And enough money to cushion the business for several slow months, should that ever happen. He knew Scolari or Lang would keep him informed about Harold's situation, and there was a good chance he'd be called to testify, which was fine with him. It was a good feeling knowing someone like Harold would be behind bars for a long, long time, and he helped to put him there. Elise had her life back. The good guys still do win some of the time. He was whistling by the time he walked into his office back in Brookfield.

"Boy, am I glad to see you!" Kelly said as he walked in the door and was greeted by an exuberant Rudy, who immediately needed his head scratched, his ears rubbed and a belly rub.

"What's up?" Zach said with a smile, his good mood still lingering.

"You need to get all your loose ends wrapped up, because after that you're going to be tied up for a few weeks," she said with a wicked grin.

"Got a juicy case for me to sink my teeth into?" Zach asked.

"Something like that," Kelly said, still smiling.

"Okay, I give up, what have you gotten me into now?" Zach asked, his interest piqued.

"You're going on a nice rustic vacation, all expenses paid, for three full weeks!" Kelly told him.

"What? Where? Who's paying for me to go on vacation, and what if I don't want to go?" Zach said, surprised by her answer.

"So many questions! Oh, you won't be able to resist, believe me. Let me ask you one question, do you have any Indiana Jones blood in you? It might come in handy." Kelly laughed as she stood up to leave. "I'm going home now, have a nice weekend. Here's some reading material for you," she said as she handed him an envelope containing several pages she had printed off. Zach could still hear her laughing as she walked out the office door.

THE END

AFTERWORD

I hope you enjoyed this book. I'm having a lot of fun writing them! NOT MY LIFE is the second in my Zachary Marchand Mystery series. If you haven't already read it, you might enjoy the first book, DEAD SERIOUS DAY. Watch for the third book in the series in late fall of 2015.

I would greatly appreciate any review you can write for me, on Amazon.

Sign up for my newsletter on my website, at www.paulettemorrissey.com and you'll be notified whenever I add new stories to this series, or write other books. There's also some fun things and free stories on my site that you may enjoy. I periodically add some of my short writings to my web site - things that haven't been published anywhere. You can also have a look at the artwork I like to create when I'm not writing.

Thanks again for taking the time to read my book! If you enjoyed it, please tell others about it.

If you didn't, please tell me!

Paulette Morrissey

www.ingramcontent.com/pod-product-compliance
Lightning Source LLC
Chambersburg PA
CBHW030321180626
46810CB00003B/1177